THE END OF THE WORLD IS ELSEWHERE

Fragments of the World IV

Essential Translations Series 56

~

Canada Council   Conseil des Arts
for the Arts   du Canada

ONTARIO ARTS COUNCIL
CONSEIL DES ARTS DE L'ONTARIO

an Ontario government agency
un organisme du gouvernement de l'Ontario

Canadä

Guernica Editions Inc. acknowledges the support of
the Canada Council for the Arts and the Ontario Arts Council.
The Ontario Arts Council is an agency of the Government of Ontario.
We acknowledge the financial support of the Government of Canada
through the National Translation Program for Book Publishing,
an initiative of the *Roadmap for Canada's Official Languages 2013–2018:
Education, Immigration, Communities,* for our translation activities.
We acknowledge the financial support of the Government of Canada.
Nous reconnaissons l'appui financier du gouvernement du Canada.

THE END OF THE WORLD IS ELSEWHERE

Fragments of the World IV

Hélène Rioux

Translated by
Jonathan Kaplansky

GUERNICA
EDITIONS
TORONTO · CHICAGO · BUFFALO · LANCASTER (U.K.)
2022

Original title: *Le bout du monde existe ailleurs* (2019)
Copyright © 2019, Leméac Éditeur inc.
Translation copyright © 2022 Jonathan Kaplansky
and Guernica Editions Inc.

Guernica Founder: Antonio D'Alfonso

Michael Mirolla, editor
David Moratto, cover and interior design
Guernica Editions Inc.
287 Templemead Drive, Hamilton (ON), Canada L8W 2W4
2250 Military Road, Tonawanda, N.Y. 14150-6000 U.S.A.
www.guernicaeditions.com

Distributors:
Independent Publishers Group (IPG)
600 North Pulaski Road, Chicago IL 60624
University of Toronto Press Distribution (UTP)
5201 Dufferin Street, Toronto (ON), Canada M3H 5T8
Gazelle Book Services, White Cross Mills
High Town, Lancaster LA1 4XS U.K.

First edition.
Printed in Canada.

Legal Deposit—Third Quarter
Library of Congress Catalog Card Number: 2022931482
Library and Archives Canada Cataloguing in Publication
Title: The end of the world is elsewhere / Hélène Rioux ; translated by
Jonathan Kaplansky.
Other titles: Bout du monde existe ailleurs. English
Names: Rioux, Hélène, 1949- author. |
Kaplansky, Jonathan, 1960- translator.
Series: Rioux, Hélène, 1949- Fragments of the world. |
Essential translations series ; 56.
Description: Series statement: Essential translations series ; 56 |
Fragments of the world ; IV |
Translation of: Le bout du monde existe ailleurs.
Identifiers: Canadiana (print) 20220157375 |
Canadiana (ebook) 20220157456 | ISBN 9781771837613 (softcover) |
ISBN 9781771837620 (EPUB)
Classification: LCC PS8585.I46 B6813 2022 | DDC C843/.54—dc23

For my friends Christine Champagne
and Hans-Jürgen Greif,
for their unwavering support.

Contents

1

The *End of the World*, Early Morning

If it snows today, if it rains buckets, what does it matter? The end of the world is elsewhere, in other climates.

Call it a childhood dream.

FOR SOME, THE word is, and has always been, a synonym for a dream. It has been that way since the world began. They have only to hear it for the desire to emerge. A spark immediately ignites in their eyes. They have only to hear it, to read it in a book. Or just to think it. Especially when things are going badly. But even when everything is going well. In the best of worlds, as Voltaire described with his legendary irony. He didn't believe in it, of course, how would he have believed in it? Our world was not, has never been, the best, far from it. And that explains perhaps why the idea arises as soon as the word is heard or read, as soon as it is uttered. A peal of thunder sounds, lightning flashes in a cloudless sky. The rainbow appears: it is a promise.

Elsewhere. The magic word, laden with all fantasies. A better world exists. Elsewhere. Where the grass is greener and softer, the sky bluer, where gold sparkles in riverbeds. Elsewhere, always farther, beyond futile borders. Think of Ulysses, of Sinbad in *The Thousand and One*

1

Nights, of Marco Polo, of Cook, of Magellan; remember Christopher Columbus when, on the morning of August 3, 1492 of our era, he set sail from Palos de la Frontera. It is that word and no other that he uttered on uncharted waters, Oceanus or the Ocean Sea, on highly unlikely routes.

Elsewhere.

Already I hear the skeptics and the sedentary protest. That's not it at all, they scold, shaking their heads. You are blinded by romanticism, as usual. The madness of men is the only thing to blame in this affair. Because, admit it, it's crazy to go away when you should be cultivating your own piece of land, erecting lasting monuments there. Crazy and irresponsible.

Others, less austere, will take a more nuanced approach, describe instead a kind of custom or tradition. At one time, they explain, for British dandies, for example, taking the grand tour of Europe after adolescence was an obligatory rite of passage. You had to visit the museums of the continent, gather your thoughts before its ruins, go slumming in the bordellos to then return enlightened, taking your place in the City or on the benches of Parliament. Reread the life of Byron or Shelley: you will see. Young people from rich countries still do it and you see them on the roads of exotic countries: Mongolia, India, Bolivia, their fair trade backpacks, their tattooed biceps, in running shoes or barefoot in their orthopedic sandals. They all have a telephone in hand, ready for a selfie. When they come of age, travellers agree to be called tourists, not before. They disembark from the cruise ship, step off the air-conditioned tour bus, follow their guide into these places that have marked the past, invading the islands, photographing remains, splendours, and miseries with the same telephones whose untimely ringing, often ridiculous, punctuates the murmuring of the world.

Still others brandish their history textbooks, claim that it is wars, invasions — bloodthirsty hordes that swept through with a thunderous roar, making the earth tremble beneath the galloping of their horses — drought, famine, and other calamities that incited or forced them to move what ails them elsewhere: all great migrations are thus explained. Boat people, refugees, deportees of all kinds, nothing, alas, has changed since the dawn of time. Gaunt, scrawny, starving, their puny children in their arms. They dig tunnels, pile up in foul smelling holds like the slaves who in times past were transported from one world to the other, huddling in containers, airplane baggage holds, or whatever. The survivors knock on the doors of privileged continents, Europe or America. Or else they enter without knocking. Without money or papers, with nothing other than their hunger and their terror, their tears, their horror stories to tell in their language, their hope for a less cruel life, that illusion. If these catastrophes had not swooped down upon them, they would never even have considered leaving their village. And here they are quoting the wandering Jew, the lost Canadian, humming their sad songs.

Still others speak of the Crusaders who, abandoning their castles and their land, in the Middle Ages, went to combat the enemies of God in the Holy Land. They quote the Filles du Roy, the galley slaves — did they even have a choice? Exile is always an ordeal, they insist. Exile is always painful.

3

It's true. True for tourism, for the Crusades and for migrations, for the majority who cherish the place where they were born and grew up. But we speak here of adventurers, of those who left, wind filling their sails, searching for everything and nothing, spices and silk, tea, pearls, emeralds, slaves. Or simply for the euphoria of discovery, when the heart suddenly hammers in the chest. We speak of those dreamers. They returned—when they returned—transformed, covered in honours, bearing evocative scars and gashes. They had survived. Adventurers and conquerors, often without faith or laws, their names forever punctuate our history, beacons in our night. Alexander the Great, Julius Caesar, Genghis Khan.

And the stories they told when they returned. What marvels they had seen elsewhere, over there, what extraordinary phenomena, sunken continents, cities as vast as the countries of the old world, the domes of which sparkled like a mirage beneath the sun; from afar, they looked like cities of gold. Those girls—people claimed they were virgins—with perfect bodies that could be discerned beneath their veils and who danced, at once shameless and graceful; still others, with light feet, entirely nude except for their collars, their belts of flowers, those emperors that the pagans venerated like gods incarnated on earth, those fertile fields as far as the eye could see—where there grew tubers in twisted shapes, weeds that people smoked solemnly at nightfall, grains that overcame the famines of the old world—the trees whose branches bent beneath the weight of fruits with flavours as sweet as honey. Aphrodisiacal plants, birds with multi-colour feathers, able to speak. Mermaids and unicorns, elephants, docile mastodons that children led nonchalantly on long chains, giraffes and other even more fabulous animals, hanging on lianas, upside down, tamed big cats, sleeping in gardens like in the time of Eden, does curled up between their paws. Horrors too: sea monsters with tentacles bristling with poisonous stingers, cyclops, insects whose bites are fatal, forty-foot-long snakes that swallowed their prey alive. Cruel giants, amazons, cruel as well, cannibalistic pygmies. Human sacrifices — appalling ceremonies — in temples built to honour implacable deities. The sickening smell of blood, of charred flesh rising toward the blue sky. Horrors and marvels.

They had braved all the dangers. They had gone up rivers infested with caimans and ravenous fish, and walked in the jungle, beaten their path, thrusting swords in the pervasive vegetation. They had experienced hunger, thirst, fever and delirium, fed themselves on roots and bitter leaves, on insects that they felt squirm in their mouths before being swallowed, still wriggling as they went down into the esophagus, moving around in their guts. They faced storms, when waves as high as castle ramparts beat down upon their decks, with the wind splitting their masts, tearing their sails and, with sinister cracking, the hull of their vessel threatened to break apart beneath the impact. Captain and sailors found themselves on the ocean floor or in the bellies of sharks: the outcome of their journey, if not the meaning of their dream. They were captured by barbarian tribes, had sometimes seen their companions perish slowly, tortured at the stake, heard moaning and cries echo in the night, until morning, sometimes all the entire next day. But they were also invited to feasts in the palaces of idolized kings, where, dazed by the intense scent of incense and flowers, they tasted the fruit, mangosteens and guavas, the *tumatl* whose seeds they brought back, and saw naked girls dance beneath their veils.

What does it matter, in the end, if these stories were true or not—doubtless some of them were—there were always some people to believe in them, to listen to them, to delight in them, wide-eyed. So it was that, from one heart to the next, the dream flowed like a spring, was passed on, and took hold forever.

≈ The traveller describes and, in the head of the person listening to him, a halftone image suddenly unfolds. In the captain's cabin, they see an old map spread out among navigation instruments on a mahogany table, as if straight out of a curio cabinet from some maritime museum. They recognize the sextant, the compass, the astrolabe that locates the position of the stars, the telescope. The goose feather and the ink bottle, the pipe, if indeed tobacco and its virtues—or vices—had already been discovered, the bottle of brandy three-quarters full or empty depending upon the captain's mood, the pewter tumbler, the pistol—at least one firearm of some sort—the dagger in its embroidered sheath, And then they finally see the one they wanted to see, the old seadog, the explorer, a pirate perhaps, bearded, cantankerous, his face gashed, leaning over it with a worried look. It: the map of the world.

Lying like that, the Earth is a flat surface, its two hemispheres projected side by side, as if, to better see it, to carry out an autopsy on it, it had been split by a meridian from one pole to the other. As if it had been quartered. That is how we imagine it in the past, immobile between the sky and the abyss, or lying in unstable equilibrium on the nape of the neck of Atlas, himself lying who knows where, floating in empty space, perhaps. Only the fool-hardy took the journey to the end of the horizon. Did they not know that the horizon recedes as one moves forward, that you never reach it? The horizon is an op-tical illusion, a utopia.

Some people ventured forth nevertheless, returning with new hypotheses. Their voyage led them to this wild conclusion: the Earth was a contained entity, a kind of rectangular chest set down on who knows what, a solid surface, a floor, and this container was hermetically sealed by the celestial dome which acted as a cover. As for others, people awaited their return in vain. For them, no cover; at the end of the horizon, there was only noth-ingness, and they had fallen into it. Shivers ran up spines when those who remained in the country imagined this fall into the great void. Do you fall eternally, and if not, when and where do you stop?

At present, the Earth is round and blue, we know: we've seen it in photos, it's part of a system, it turns among a multitude of stars in an infinite sky. And this very sky is perhaps not unique in its kind; perhaps others exist, identical or not—go figure how many—in other spaces just as infinite. Our galaxy is scarcely more than an atom in a limitless body constantly expanding.

Which is hardly more reassuring, you must admit. Before, we were the pole of attraction. Sun—one sole sun —stars and Moon turning without ever tiring around our immobile Earth. Chosen by God, our planet attracted them like a magnet. We were all, alpha and omega, prom-ised to eternity, paradise or Gehenna.

We are, in the end, insignificant, and the ego has suffered a great blow. We thought we were unique, created in the image of a God who, severe as he is benevolent, watches over us as if over his children. From now on, it is Big Brother watching us and judging us, condemning us or saving us. We were destined to a hereafter of glory or sorrow, but to eternity rather than nothingness. Here we are regressing, like those sudden hurricanes reduced to ordinary tropical storms. Life used to have meaning and, viewed from that perspective, our ordeals seemed more bearable, explainable, at least. We believed in justice; we qualified it as immanent. We now know our insignificance: we have not been chosen, we will not be eternal. Dust, we will return to dust. That is our fate, and it is sad.

Some will say so much the better. Others, thinking over their dreary or unhappy lives, their errors, the missed opportunities, their cowardice, will remember the shame, yes, the shame, nevertheless buried deep in an obscure recess of their memory, and will regret that a second chance was not given to them to atone for the one they ruined.

≈ So that cabin, and that map of the world — dotted with grey areas — spread out on a work table in scratched mahogany. Words in Latin, names of seas, oceans, lands known or not, are carefully traced in black ink on the parchment. On the oldest map recorded — dating from five centuries before our era — that of Anaximander, never found, but recreated based on old manuscripts, three continents make up the world; the Aegean Sea is the centre. In the other still unsuspected hemisphere,

China—Cathay—boasted, it too, of being the centre of the universe, the Middle Kingdom.

The vessel we imagine, galleon or caravel, we nevertheless prefer it in the middle of the Atlantic, the Ocean Sea, rather than in the *mare nostrum*, as the Romans called the Mediterranean. We want it propelled toward an America still to be discovered and pillaged.

A lighted candle diffuses its meagre light upon this décor. Night has long fallen, the sky is black, no stars; the vessel sails on a shadowy sea. Drunken, this vessel, like that of the poet? But Rimbaud did not sail on the sea; he went down rivers, the Amazon, most likely, or perhaps even the St. Lawrence, why not, the Rio Grande, or the Mississippi, an American river. Because America had been discovered three and a half centuries earlier; it was not the Eldorado; Rimbaud's ship sank like Aguirre in his colourful heart.

Let's say that the ship left Saint-Malo, that it left Genoa or Cadiz at the summer solstice. Autumn had begun and the horizon continued to recede, without ever revealing anything. The navigator, a visionary, nevertheless sought another route, faster and more certain, to fabulous India, to Cathay, and when he returned to port, for he did not doubt he would return, his ship would be filled with spices, porcelain, and silk. Gold especially, another word that ignited sparks in people's eyes. He knew that his sponsors who remained there were expecting riches and seething with impatience. But he lost his way, no Asia—no hope—emerged and the exhausted crew grew discontented. The captain did not want to give up; he knew, or guessed, sensed that, like everything down here, the ocean had an end, that a world exists at the end. He stood firm despite the grim looks, full of anger and resentment, that the sailors gave him. Some died during the crossing, of scurvy, dysentery, of fights that turned out badly, their bodies thrown into the sea after the priest's blessing. The captain stood firm. For how long?

* * *

Marjolaine looks up, places her cup on the saucer. A waiter, coffeepot in hand, all smiles — they always smile — approaches her table. She indicates no, and closes her book.

The life of Christopher Columbus, five hundred and thirty-two pages, not one less. She read it in scarcely eight days, a first for her. Because between work, home, and the family, she never had much time to devote to reading. Busy all day, too tired when evening came. Perhaps she didn't want to either. But all that is going to change. To start with, she registered as a member at her local library, in Little Italy. The first book she selected was a novel she wanted to read on the cruise. The title had misled her. And the purple orchid on the glossy cover. You mustn't go by appearances, as well she knows, having learned it at her own expense and on more than one occasion. While the back cover had not told her much — the author, a Finn with an unpronounceable name, had already published a half dozen bestsellers — the title had intrigued her. *The Pirate and the Orchid* had suggested romantic, even fantastic adventures, with attacks, hidden treasure on an island, a femme fatale, and a damsel in distress. The seductive pirate especially, as pitiless as he was courageous. To make the journey in style, on the wings of a dream. To fill the hours of solitude, for that's what there would be. But none of that in this story. The orchid was the name of a cannibalistic sect at the ends of Indonesia, in the jungle, and the novel began with the description of its macabre rituals. Some details were bone-chilling—and Marjolaine had felt her blood run cold. Cannibals! They had them in Cuba too; Christopher Columbus had described them in his letters to the kings of Spain; she would never have believed it. She spent a week there with Marcel last year, for their twentieth wedding anniversary. In summer—less expensive. It had rained the whole time, a bit sad, even in a four-star hotel. As for the food, no point in mentioning it. But the Cubans were delightfully kind. The descendants of cannibals? Hard to imagine. To consume one's fellow creatures when there were all those exotic fruits, all those birds, all those fish. You had only to reach out your arm, throw your nets into the sea. To think about it, perhaps there were even some in Canada, who knows? When they bound missionaries to the stake, perhaps they ate them afterwards. She looks at the croissant she's started on: in her plate the raspberry jam resembles coagulated blood and suddenly she's no longer hungry. Incredible, what you can come up with to torment your fellow man. As for the pirate in the novel, he had yet to appear when she closed the book. But she no longer wanted to meet him: she'd read thirty pages and had had enough. She went to the ship's library and Béatrice was there. It was she who gave her Christopher Columbus.

It's such a small world. She scarcely believed her eyes when she recognized the passenger. A customer from the

End of the World, the restaurant where she herself had been a waitress and then a cook for about fifteen years. This one would often arrive in the evening to meet up with the tea drinker, a regular. They hadn't seen her in a while. There, on the ship, she was limping a bit. But it was her; impossible to make a mistake.

Marjolaine leaves the dining room, practically deserted at this hour. True, she rises early, a deeply rooted habit. In Montreal, it was always at six o'clock; she doesn't need an alarm clock, her biological clock never lets her down. She makes coffee, Marcel's lunch, breakfast for her teenagers—it's as if she spends her life cooking. But now, on the ship, she forces herself to spend at least one hour more in bed, daydreaming. After all, she is on vacation. She heads toward the deck. Most of the passengers are still asleep; they celebrated until late in the night and it's as if she had the ship to herself.

The cruise is drawing to an end. Tonight, the last one they'll spend on board, is the fall equinox. Ten days at sea, the Aegean, on a ship that is also called *End of the World*—the name is written in black italics on its spotless hull. A white ship with elegant lines, a floating palace.

The passengers come from all over, speak in languages with guttural or hushing sounds. Leaving from Venice, they made brief stops in the islands: Delos and Mykonos, Paros, Naxos, and Santorini, places whose existence Marjolaine hadn't known about until then. It hadn't rained one single day; not a drop fell from the cloudless sky. She thought she was dreaming. Perhaps earthly paradise is here—Christopher Columbus believed in it. He looked for it too far. Sometimes happiness is within arm's reach. Now she is overcome by a wave of melancholy: she thinks of Marcel, of their children remaining over there, is angry with herself for enjoying privileges she has not shared with them.

The trip is coming to an end and she still has the impression of floating. They will dock in the port of Piraeus, this time, tomorrow morning. One day in Athens, with a few activities planned: visiting historical sites and an evening in a typical restaurant in the Plaka featuring a traditional menu and folk dances. She promises herself to take advantage of it. In Venice, she was too tired. Then, the day after tomorrow, the airplane to Montreal, a ten-hour flight. When she returns, she'll tell them about all she's seen during her journey, all she's learned. She sees them already, Marcel and the children, her friends, Laure perhaps, Denise, surely, and the others sitting in her living room and listening to her, wide-eyed. When she tells them, for example, that the most ancient habitats in the Cyclades date from thirty centuries before Christ. Three thousand years, yes, before Christ, if indeed Jesus was really born when they said he was. The world is small, but also so old—and life is so short. She's eager to go home, and, at the same time, wishes the journey would never end. Because returning is coming back to things the way she left them; they will not have changed during her absence. It was John Paradis who told her that. John Paradis, a Québécois like Béatrice and her. The three of them always eat together.

Easy for him to say that. A retired university professor, he has no money worries, that's obvious. Besides, the things he left behind, waiting, he does not often find again. He's been touring, gallivanting around, as he says, for close to six months; he went as far as Russia. Apparently in St. Petersburg in summer, the sun does not set before midnight.

"That's where the great Pushkin died," he said, his voice quavering.

"Poutine died?"

He rolled his eyes.

"No, not Poutine. Pushkin, Marjolaine. A great poet."

Sometimes he makes her dizzy. She is naïve, she knows, she lacks culture, but is not stupid. Not everyone has had the opportunity to go to university. It is as if he forgets that.

He said that after the cruise he intends to stop off in Vienna. He wants to see Mayerling, where an archduke died—in the end, the world is a vast cemetery. Assassination or suicide, the affair was never cleared up. A light went on in Marjolaine's brain. She understood what he was talking about.

"Suicide," she said. "With the wife he loved. I know, I saw the film early in the summer."

Since being unemployed, she has lots of time to watch TV. There's a station on cable that shows old movies, often in black and white, all day long. That's how she saw *Mayerling* with Charles Boyer.

"Because you think that movies always tell the truth?"

"His name was Rudolf, and hers ... Marie. And yes, I believe in them."

"Mary, Mary Vetsera. But the truth, Marjolaine, was never known. They spoke of a duel, of a crime of passion or political crime, and of suicide also, for all kinds of contradictory motives. History is not an exact science, fortunately."

She raised her eyebrows.

"What do you mean, fortunately?"

"Fortunately, because that's how people can continue researching: nothing is definite. Whatever the cause, the event was the prelude to the fall of the Austrian-Hungarian empire. And to the First World War, of course."

Of course.

"Did you know that Adolf Hitler was born two hundred and fifty kilometres from there three months later?"

She did not know that.

The sea is as calm as a lake. A great deal of wind this week, but this morning it let off, and the ship seems to be rocking itself.

≈ Actually, for Marjolaine, all of it, the cruise, the ship, the Greek islands, began with a nightmare or almost when, last July, the End of the World — that is another End of the World, the greasy spoon where she toiled like a slave, on Rue Saint-Zotique in La Petite-Patrie — was about to close for renovations and Jean-Charles Dupont, the owner, suddenly informed her that she would not be coming back. He didn't put it that bluntly, but for her it was crystal clear: she was a part of the old things they were getting rid of. After fifteen and a half years of loyal service, and for starvation wages yet, they were tossing her out like an old rag. Not even in the recycling bin, straight into the garbage. You have to wonder what the point of loyalty is. Had the sky fallen on her head, she could not have been more stunned. Knocked senseless. Gratitude, like many other words — justice, freedom — is a word void of meaning. If she hadn't known that, she would have learned it at her own expense that evening.

To be fair to Dupont: he seemed to have a heavy heart as he informed her of the news. It was eleven thirty; she'd finished her day or evening of work, everything was shining in the cubbyhole that served as a kitchen, the dishes washed, the night's offerings—Chinese macaroni, stuffed green peppers, turkey (the leftovers from the day before) to be served as is (the holiday special) or à la king on a vol-au-vent, carrot coins, peas, mashed potatoes, everything ready to be heated—the lettuce spun, three quarters of a marble cake under the plastic dome, the goblets of mango Jell-O, a new flavour she wanted to try out, and butterscotch pudding in the fridge. For the "chiffonade gaspésienne," a name invented by Louison, she'd mixed three large cans of pink salmon with mayonnaise, diced celery, shallots—oops, green onions—and parsley. All that remained was to set the concoction on lettuce leaves, surround with tomatoes and pre-sliced radishes, and top it with a stuffed olive. Nothing too complicated. She planned to go home and have a cup of tea on the porch with Marcel if he hadn't already gone to bed. He works in construction and, in summer, the days are long on the building sites.

Strange how all that is clear in her memory; there are moments like that which are imprinted forever. Marjolaine remembers the slightest detail; it's as if the scene had taken place yesterday. She must have played it over a hundred, a thousand times in her head, inventing all the replies she hadn't said: it's always after the fact that we find what would have allowed us to shut up the enemy, reduce him to nothingness. The program *Romantic Cities* had just started on the radio. A vocalist was singing at the top of her lungs in English about the charms of New York. On the silent TV, a disputed tennis match from early that evening in Jarry Park was being rebroadcast. The restaurant was deserted. Gabriela, the waitress, had left a few minutes earlier; the nighttime regulars—taxi drivers who stopped long enough to gulp down a meal on the run, young people who were famished after the neighbourhood bars closed and other insomniacs—had not yet arrived. Had there been people there, she would have of course remained until the owner's son came to relieve her at midnight. She did that often, not even counting the overtime. As meek as they come, a pushover, sometimes people murmured about her behind her back.

But there was not a trace of a customer, and Jean-Charles Dupont was going to guard the fort. So she'd removed her apron, picked up her purse and was almost at the door when Dupont called her back. He placed two glasses on the counter, and a bottle of cognac—an innovation of Louison—the one they sold at eight dollars for a thimbleful, a finger, not a micro-millimetre more she insisted, tax and service not included. But, at that price, no one ever ordered any.

"A small drop, Marjolaine?" he'd proposed. "For the road, as they say."

She didn't know they said that. How would she have? In any case, drinking cognac with the boss was a first. A coffee, a beer at the most discussing the week's menus—always the same ones, in fact, it reassured the customers, always the same as well—events that had disturbed their daily routine. And they had more than their share of them in the last year: Doris' death in the bathroom, for example, an aneurism while the others played their game of five hundred, an extension of euchre. Nine months ago today the tragedy occurred, nine months to the day, Marjolaine suddenly realizes and her heart stops beating for a moment. Not to mention the time when Raoul Potvin burned Diderot Toussaint's winning lottery ticket. An incomprehensible act, even if had tried to justify it with an explanation too lame to be believed: he and Diderot, both taxi drivers, were associates, it appeared: they'd bought their lottery tickets together for years without ever winning anything. Diderot had betrayed him when he surreptitiously bought one for himself alone. Marjolaine hasn't come close to forgetting the commotion that followed the auto-da-fé. No, it's not because you're in a small neighbourhood restaurant that nothing ever happens. Finally there had been the boss' request for divorce, the arrival of Louison, his new flame, who turned everything upside down; that is her arrival upon the scene led to the separation of the couple united for better or for worse for twenty-five years. That Louison was stuck up, snobbish, and underhanded. What on earth did he find in her? Not even that pretty, to Marjolaine's mind. Not a natural beauty, in any case. Reconstructed, redone from head to toe at great expense in private clinics. Marjolaine had been wary of her from the start, as had Laure and Denise. But that was a topic that the boss had never addressed.

So, the cognac and the glasses. On the radio, a singer whimpered that Capri was "fini." Monsieur Dupont had a guilty conscience, that was clear. He beat around the bush for a good half hour speaking of this and that, the renovations they would do this summer, the turquoise back wall and the whole shebang, the big mirror behind the bar "to give the impression of depth" — for from now on it would be a bar, gone would be the days of the good old scratched counter where the loners liked to sit and chat with the waitress while drinking their coffee — the vintage stools. "You know all that is going to cost me a fortune, Marjolaine." And she, none too clever, nodded her head, feigned enthusiasm and acquiesced, not suspecting a thing. Unaware of the famous sword of Damocles hanging over her heard. She even made a few suggestions.

"Why not parlour games? Organizing tournaments, perhaps? This has always been a place where people like to play. At home I have dominos, checkers as well; I could bring them if you like."

And he:

"That's an idea, Marjolaine. We'll think about it."

"We," excluding as it often does the person who spoke, was of course Louison.

And then the cat was out of the bag. They always end up getting out. Impossible otherwise: shut up for too long in a bag, they would not survive.

That guilty look on his face as he filled her glass for the third time, with her protesting: "No, no, I'm not used to drinking, you know full well. And tired from working all day ..." She can imagine the expression on Marcel's face were she to come home loaded. Because her vision was starting to blur, things around her were swaying. What did he want? To get her drunk before taking advantage of her?

Instead it was to deal the final blow, and the cognac at eight dollars a sip, a drop, was indeed the last drink of the condemned. For that's when he opened his briefcase

—lying on the counter next to the bottle—rummaged in his papers, removed a sealed white envelope and handed it to her. He cleared his throat. The cat was out of the bag and now he appeared to be tongue tied.

"It's not a lot, Marjolaine, a small token, if you will. Of my ... my ... friendship. My gratitude, I mean."

"Gratitude?"

"For all these wonderful years that you had the kind ... kindness to give us."

"I just did my job."

"Yes, and you did it very well, Marjolaine ... This is called severance pay."

She acted as if she didn't understand. In fact, she didn't understand. Or didn't want to understand. Her head was spinning.

"What do you mean, severance? Is somebody leaving?"

That forced him to explain. In this case, leaving meant dismissal, and he was referring to hers. It was not his decision, at least not entirely, not exactly. If it were only up to him, she would remain. She must know that. He had absolutely no criticism of her.

"But, you understand, for the End of the World, Louison has ideas, plans ... for which your ... your style, your style of cooking, I mean, and I enjoy it, please don't think, I've enjoyed it for years, especially your shepherd's pie, of course I will miss it ... for which your style of cooking is not suited—anymore, I mean. Canadian cooking ... as we used to call it, is no longer suitable. The neighbourhood has changed, you know as well as I; it's become gentrified and people now have other requirements. More refined. We must adapt, if not we'll go bankrupt."

That stilted way of expressing himself. As if he'd

memorized the text—written by Louison of course—and was trying to recite it as best he could. It couldn't have been easy; the bravura performance stuck in his throat. He stammered. In the background, a nostalgic tune: Beau Dommage sang its lament about Montreal. Marjolaine looked up at the television. One of the players, the one with the yellow headband in his hair—a Spaniard who made Gabriela swoon—brandished his racket, looking determined to crush everything around him.

"To tell the truth, Louison has found a young chef, a graduate of the Institut d'hôtellerie, who, apparently, is second to none when it comes to tapas and zakuskis."

The last sentence, the conclusion, came out in one breath, in one go.

"The director of the Institut is a client of Louison," he said.

Because the traitor sold houses as well.

A kind of Pontius Pilate who washes her hands when the time comes to deliver the blow. In any case, she didn't understand a word of what he was saying. She'd never heard of zakuskis. What were they, exactly? Flying fish? Prickly tropical fruit? She still doesn't know and doesn't care.

She opened the envelope of pain and misery, hands trembling. Inside was a cheque in a carefully folded white sheet. She had to take her glasses to decipher the amount written in a spidery scrawl. Four thousand dollars.

"We're closing in a week," Monsieur Dupont said as if nothing had happened, clearly relieved now that the damage was done. "I could have waited until the last minute to give it to you. But I preferred to be alone just the two of us ... Louison doesn't know about the amount."

Because surely she would have found it exorbitant. "Come on, Charlou—she called him Charlou—it's just the cook, half, even one quarter would have more than enough. If that." That's what she would have said in her high-pitched voice. Marjolaine felt, still feels, as if she can hear her. Whereas bankers, managers and other crooks receive millions when they bow out after swindling the public.

Four thousand dollars was in fact a lot of money. Nevertheless, she almost tore the cheque into pieces. She was not for sale. She decided otherwise, fortunately.

He said that if she chose to not return to work for the last week, he'd understand. He'd pay her just the same.

"It's up to you. And don't worry. We'll manage. Even I know how to make poutine."

Was this a joke? He smiled sheepishly—a two-faced smile. Not her.

"A polite way of saying I'm not indispensable?"

"Not at all, Marjolaine, No. You know full well that ..."

"Well, no, in fact, I don't."

He swallowed his last sip of cognac.

"I understand that it's not easy. For me either, believe me."

Believe him?

"Liar!" she wanted to shout. But not another sound would come out of her mouth. A lump in her throat.

"If you'd rather, I can send you the forms for unemployment in the mail," he hastened to add. "You'll receive it for a year; that will give you time to prepare. And if you want a reference ..."

She did not reply.

"Otherwise I can bring them to you at home myself. The forms. I'll place them in your mailbox. Or, if you like, I can help you fill them out."

Did he take her for an illiterate?

The purr of his voice. He gave her one final piece of advice. Friendly advice, he clarified.

"Take advantage of this break to register for courses, Marjolaine. In nouvelle cuisine, for example. It's never too late. You have potential, believe me."

The program *Romantic Cities* was about to end. One hour, not even, to settle her fate. An execution quickly carried out, very clean, flawless, like those supposedly intelligent missiles they talked about on the news during the Gulf War. And now, Charles Aznavour—Venice that was sad. A cult song that listeners requested at least once a month. To think they would all drown their romantic disappointments in its polluted lagoon. She had a vision of gondolas gliding along canals of salty tears.

Venice was not alone in being sad that evening. Marjolaine seemed to be on the verge of bursting into tears. Monsieur Dupont offered to drive her home. She refused. Out of the question to give him the satisfaction of seeing her break down, the pleasure of trying to console her. One has one's dignity. Besides, it was a way for him to crash into a lamppost, with his blood alcohol level, for them to both find themselves in emergency with three broken ribs or worse. Boris Savine, the taxi driver, had just entered. She said: "He will drive me home." She folded the cheque, tucked it away in her purse, stood up, took Boris by the arm, and led him, dumbfounded, to the exit without giving him the time to order his coffee.

In the taxi, her nerves gave way; she began to sob.

When they reached her place, Boris, both upset and appalled, didn't want to take any money. "The dirty dog. The bastard," he said, fists clenched. And other words, maybe in Russian. "You can be sure I'll never set foot in there again. Nor will my brother."

≈ But Marjolaine had not cried for long. She slept on it, and the next morning made her decision. Marcel also slept on it, had a few ideas about how to spend the money. He alluded to it at breakfast.

"I was thinking that a new car …"

A car? Marjolaine remained silent.

"I'm not talking about a new car," he said, retracting immediately. "But with our four thousand and what they'll give us for our Honda …"

What did he mean, "our" four thousand?

"It's still good enough, the Honda."

"It's already seven years old. That's not new for a car … Okay then, an alarm system? Lately there've been robberies in the neighbourhood."

"I don't see what they could want to steal from us."

"An air conditioning system, what do you think? When there's a heatwave, with the smog and pollution, you can hardly breathe in Montreal."

But, for once, the submissive wife who always said yes said no. Heatwaves occur one week a year, ten days at the most, and some years there's not even a summer. She was through with generosity: she'd given enough. The money was hers alone, she had certainly earned it with the sweat of her brow in the un-air-conditioned kitchen, feet swollen from remaining standing for hours in front of her stove, not to mention the shooting pains in her back at the end of the day. She had indeed earned the money, and it was hers to blow. "The boss said it was severance pay. Well, I'm going away." It was more than time: fifteen years at the End of the World without ever leaving La Petite-Patrie, other than—aside from the vacation in Cuba—a weekend up North when Marcel went fishing—the mosquitoes and the deerflies ate them up alive. After a couple of these expeditions, she'd given up.

The most incredible thing was that she wanted to go away alone. No one could believe it. Marcel, their two children, the regulars at the restaurant—Diderot, Laure, Denise, Boris, his brother Feder—they were all dumbfounded, "Call it a childhood dream," she said, justifying herself. "And you don't share a dream. Aside from our sorrows, it's the only thing that belongs to us." The moment had come to fulfil one, before it was too late. Of course she was thinking of all the times that Doris had spoken to her of California, her dream, Los Angeles, Santa Monica, especially Hollywood, where you can come across legendary stars, actors and actresses at every step on Sunset Boulevard, and who had passed away in the bathroom of a small restaurant on Rue Saint-Zotique without ever getting on a plane. The farthest the poor woman had gone was to Niagara Falls, the honeymoon of a marriage that hadn't lasted.

That was how she told everything, in those words or almost, to Béatrice in the ship's library on the third day of the cruise.

There was something else, however, something she kept to herself: she did not want, or could not face, to be in the vicinity when the new End of the World, renovated, spruced up, sophisticated, opened its doors with its chef, second to none, its exotic recipes, and its large mirror behind the bar. The opening was planned for September 21, Charlou Dupont's birthday. This evening, in fact. And come to think of it, it was also that evening that the weekly card games would start up again. They were held every Wednesday evening in the back room of the restaurant. Six players: three forlorn women, Doris, Laure, Denise; three taxi drivers, Diderot, Boris, Raoul Potvin. Doris' death had interrupted the ritual. From now on, the players would meet at Denise's place. Marjolaine and Marcel would take part.

To return to the opening of the restaurant, she knows herself; she would not have been able to stop herself from going to see and it would only have aggravated the wound. Because regardless of the result, failure or success, she would have been excluded. And there's the rub.

They must have put up posters in the neighbourhood to announce the event, she now thinks. Or else they sent invitations, and only their close friends and relatives will be at the celebration. She wonders where they are at with the preparations. What time is it, over there? A seven-hour time difference between Montreal and the Cyclades. So it's the middle of the night. Are they sleeping? She thinks not. Must be pandemonium. Perhaps they're having flowers delivered to place on the tables. Or candles of all colours. And what if one of them falls, if the tablecloths catch fire and the whole restaurant burns down? That thought snatches a smile from her. She knows there will be an upright piano in the back room, the one whose wall will now be turquoise. Denise learned that from Gabriela —she they kept, to clear away the tables, and bring water and coffee. Vanessa—the boss' daughter (he has three children)—will play; she's talented. Marjolaine hopes that it rains buckets, that there is a power failure, that their fiesta is a complete flop. That the young chef has broken a leg. Was scalded. Or Louison. Yes, Louison, that's even better. She imagines her, in a comforting vision, slipping on a banana peel and falling face first into the pot of mushroom soup. Oops, porcini velouté, that's what you have to call it now.

The song about Venice has remained in her head; it was to Venice that she would go to begin. And out of the question for it to be sad. So, when she saw that advertisement in the Travel section of her Saturday newspaper —"Greek Island Cruise aboard the *End of the World*, departs Venice September 12"—she understood it as a sign of destiny, a revelation.

"There is an end of the world elsewhere," she proclaimed, to whoever wanted to hear it. "And that's where I'm going."

That is how Marjolaine went from the End of the World on Rue Saint-Zotique to the one on the Aegean Sea.

2

Reunion at Denise's Place

... it was also this evening that the weekly card games would start up again. Doris' death had interrupted them. From now on, the players would meet at Denise's place.

THEY HAVE BEEN cooking since morning. It will be the holiday special, like in the golden days of the old End of the World, when Marjolaine cooked there and the classic meal was offered twenty-four hours a day every day of the year or almost: roasted turkey with the trimmings: potatoes, green peas and cranberries, gravy, stuffing and giblets. Not to mention the pot of vegetable soup, the tourtière, and the pies—sugar, apple, lemon meringue. All that despite the heatwave Montreal has been under even though it's the end of September. This afternoon, between two and three o'clock, the mercury climbed to thirty-six degrees, forty-four with the humidex factor, and a smog advisory was repeated on the radio every hour. To hear them, you'd think that just breathing was dangerous for the health. It is, undoubtedly: the air is teeming with bacteria, filth, and carbon who knows what. Oxides. They warn people to stay home as much as possible and to drink a lot of water. As if there weren't bacteria in the water. Although the blades of the ceiling fan are turning at top speed, they only shift the heavy, suffocating air around. In this heat, the smell of food becomes almost sickening. Denise and Laure are sweating heavily in the kitchen. A bad idea, in the end, the holiday special; they would have been better off sticking to simple things: salads and tomato sandwiches and ice cream for dessert. But a promise is a promise. And Marjolaine too cooked six days out of seven without ever complaining, regardless of the weather.

The men will bring the beer.

Françoise, who will replace her sister Doris, has just arrived to lend a hand, as promised. She brought her grandson, Lulu, one year old, and that was not planned.

"You'll have to excuse me if I'm late. I had no choice. Stéphanie is still bickering with her good-for-nothing partner. She was in no condition to take care of the baby. Especially since he's teething."

Leaning over the stroller, Laure looks as if she's purring.

Françoise informs her that she fed him before leaving. She gave him his bath. He's already in his pyjamas, and should be good for the night. He's exhausted, she says. He wasn't able to take a nap today. And if he does wake up, she has brought him a bottle.

Irritated, Denise shrugs her shoulders. So he's in his pyjamas—yellow with multicoloured bear cubs—what difference does it make to her? He's there and that's what exasperates her.

"It was supposed to be an evening among adults," she says, grumbling.

"We'll work it out," Laure says in a conciliatory tone.

"He won't bother you," Françoise says.

For the moment, he is sleeping in his stroller, it's true.

Françoise pushes him to Denise's bedroom, returning to the kitchen after closing the door.

"This time, he appears to be gone for good," she says, touching the table—made of wood. "I'm talking about Francis, of course. But he says that every time. And when he comes back, because he always ends up coming back …"

"She falls back into his arms," Laure croons, a bit off-key.

Denise decrees that Stéphanie has only to change the locks. She grabs a vegetable peeler, begins peeling the potatoes as if resolved to skin Françoise or Stéphanie. Or Lulu.

"She says that too, every time," Françoise says. "She lacks willpower."

She must take after her mother, Denise feels like replying.

Françoise shakes her head, serves herself a glass of water from the tap.

"Would you prefer a soft drink?" Laure asks. "There's Diet Coke in the fridge. Ginger ale as well."

"No, no, just water. I'm completely dehydrated. I walked from home. I find it a bit complicated taking public transportation with the stroller. I'm not twenty anymore."

She sits down at the table, sighing.

"Stéphanie discourages me. Completely broke, cogitating inside the four walls of her hovel: that's not a life. At least not the one I'd hoped for her. Yet I did my best."

Denise throws the potatoes into a pot, rummages in the utensil drawer. She has no pity for lazy people. She worked hard, all her life, without being able to count on her drunkard of a husband. Stéphanie has only to go to work like everyone else.

"She's taking care of her little one," Françoise says. "And even if she wanted to work, what kind of job could she find? She didn't even finish high school. There's only factory work, or a cashier at a Dollarama, all that at minimum wage, not enough to pay for daycare, even subsidized. Or else a waitress in an inexpensive restaurant."

"What do you have against waitresses? Marjolaine was one, and it didn't prevent her from raising two children."

Exactly, Françoise thinks. *We see how it ended. No security in that kind of work. They throw you out when you no longer suit them.*

No, the best thing would be for her daughter to go back to school to learn a trade. Another promise. Not that she's not intelligent. But when the time comes to enrol, she can't manage to decide what she wants to study.

Denise washes the pots. Laure dries them. Françoise peels a cucumber, and then stops, peeler in the air.

"I walked by the End of the World earlier. It looks pretty nice now. I saw a turquoise wall in the back. It made me think of the Caribbean. The menu was posted in the window. I took a glance and—"

"We don't want to know," Denise says, interrupting. "And please don't mention the End of the World in front of Marcel."

"No, no," Françoise says, mortified. "I know how to behave. What do you take me for?"

≈ They are going to start up their Wednesday card games again, a tradition that has lasted for a half a dozen years, interrupted by Doris' death, which occurred nine months earlier, on December 21 in the middle of the night, during their last game of five hundred. Except that today is Thursday. The date, September 21, was chosen to commemorate the mournful event. Playing cards on the very premises where the unfortunate woman had passed on seemed sacrilegious; they hadn't dared. But the mourning period is now over. You can't spend your life crying.

"Nine months; that's the amount of time it takes to make a baby," Denise says. "It's like a birth."

She raises her glass of Diet Coke.

"To your health, my Doris. We'll see each other in paradise. Or in hell."

She bursts out laughing. Laure nods her head, smiles. But Françoise stifles a sob: after all, they're talking about her sister. That kind of lame joke is out of place, especially today. Then she rushes into the bedroom: Lulu has awakened and is demanding God knows what very loudly. He has not slept twenty minutes.

"Well, that's promising," Denise says, muttering. And then once Françoise has left the kitchen: "I don't know about you, but personally I find her rather depressing. I'm starting to wonder if it was a good idea to invite her."

"Not so loud; she'll hear you," Laure says, whispering.

"So let her hear me," Denise says, lowering her voice a little just the same.

Laure objects that it's natural that Françoise is depressed. Her sister Doris has been dead for nine months, and it's tonight that they're celebrating—is that the right word?—the tragic anniversary.

"Admit it's not much fun," she says. "She's no longer in the first bloom of youth, and with her poor health, to have to continually mind her grandson ..."

Denise nods her head without conviction. She has always refused to babysit her grandchildren. She has eight of them, nine with the one on the way, so if she'd given in, even once, she'd have been forced to do the same for the others. She has always been fair with her brood.

"In that sense ..."

Laure has no children. Took care of her parents till the end, an exemplary daughter. Afterwards, it was too late to marry. Sometimes she imagines herself on the platform of a station watching the trains go by. Hers never comes or else she has forgotten her suitcase, lost her ticket. Marjolaine wanted her to sign up on a dating site; she says that it's never too late for love. And if it is not mad passion, in the end, so much the better. She could at least meet someone with whom to enjoy spending time in restaurants, at the movies and the theatre. Laure won't do it. A plan to fall into a conman's trap. Not that she is rich, but the little that she has, she'd like to keep. A thief or even worse, a killer of women. They exist. Landru, for example. They place ads or answer them; she can't remember. In any case he killed all the ones he met like that. There are still Landrus in the world, and she certainly does not want to end up in a wood stove.

"I've already paid my dues" Denise says. "Especially since my ex, the devil take his soul, was never there to help me."

I've paid mine too, Laure thinks, but without saying so. A natural caregiver, as they now define it. She remembers her parents' last years, her mother with dementia, her father in a wheelchair. Incontinent.

"In any case, personally, if I had any, it would be my pleasure to take care of them, for sure," she says. "Family is sacred."

But Denise insists: there was never any question of Françoise bringing her grandson. She could have at least warned them.

"I would have refused, of course, and we'd have gotten along without her. And I don't know if you noticed, but she didn't even apologize."

"It seems to me she did. For having arrived late."

"But not for bringing the baby. Come to think of it, wasn't she supposed to have brought a bottle of wine? Did you see any sign of it? Not me."

"With all her problems, she must have forgotten. It's understandable."

Denise shrugs her shoulders. Laure sighs. She's afraid that this reunion, for which they have gone to so much trouble, will end badly. It has already happened more than once. *Fine*, she thinks. *What's done is done; there is no point on going back over it. They're not very well going to bicker like when Raoul Potvin was there.*

Denise opens the oven door, checks on the turkey, sticking her fork into the thigh of the bird.

"Almost done; we're going to enjoy it. At least there's that."

She looks at her watch.

"Six-twenty. The men must be going to show up soon. They're supposed to be here between six-thirty and seven. I hope they'll be hungry even in this heat."

"I wouldn't worry about that. If you want my opinion,

there is no temperature that would spoil their appetite. Men, especially those guys, are always starving."

As if an old maid, and a virgin, Denise would swear to it, knew anything about men's appetites.

In the bedroom, the baby continues to shout at the top of his lungs.

They hear Françoise cooing little sounds to try to soothe him to no avail. Denise lifts the cover of a pot, sets it down noisily on the counter and grabs the potato masher as if it were a weapon.

"Would you set the table while I mash the potatoes? I don't get the impression we can count on Gramma to help us. We may as well get on with it."

*　*　*

Boris Savine arrived at the appointed time with Marcel, Marjolaine's husband, who is replacing Raoul Potvin, excluded—and never seen again—since the burned lottery ticket incident. As if he too had gone up in smoke, and no one is complaining. For this evening, Françoise will replace Doris. But just for this evening. Once she returns from her trip, Marjolaine will take over.

The men have brought a case of twenty-four, half lager, half red. Marcel says that they'll have more delivered from the corner store if needed.

Boris nods his head toward the bedroom, where the concert of howling and cooing is going full blast.

"Have you opened a daycare?"

Denise rolls her eyes to the ceiling.

"Françoise showed up with her daughter's kid. Without even consulting us."

"He's teething; that's why he's crying," Laure says. "He's a good baby, usually."

"What would you know about it?"

Laure sighs.

"I'll bring him his bottle," she says without answering the question.

She opens the refrigerator door.

"It will calm him down."

Boris' cell phone begins buzzing in the pocket of his white and grey striped polo shirt. When Laure returns to the kitchen, the cries have stopped.

Boris puts the phone back in his pocket. Toussaint is going to be late, he announces. Caught in a traffic jam on Boulevard Métropolitain. He says not to wait for him to eat.

Denise is concerned: the turkey is more than cooked now; it will dry out if it remains in the oven too long.

Françoise returns and proclaims that all is well. Lulu will go to sleep drinking from his bottle. She's settled him up on the bed between two pillows. No danger of him falling. She's closed the venetian blinds.

"He's not going to wet the mattress, I hope?"

"Don't worry about that. I put him on a towel."

Denise starts. But Françoise reassures her. A towel that she's brought from home.

Marcel proposes drinking a beer to begin. But in the living room. They're dying of the heat in the kitchen.

Denise wants to go take a quick shower. Her blouse is sticking to her back. Because in addition to the forty degrees it must be in the kitchen, she's having hot flashes. None of which improves her mood.

≈ Sitting on the olive-green couch, Marcel looks morose.

"If he gets here too late, we won't have any time to play."

"We've always found time," Boris says. "Just ask Marjolaine when she returns."

"Yeah ... but I start tomorrow morning at seven."

"Speaking of Marjolaine, have you any news?" Laure asks.

"How would I? She's on a ship, and she's never learned how the Internet works. She'll be back the day after tomorrow; that's all that I know."

Denise, her hair wet, in a pink floral dress—the one that was hanging on a hanger in the bathroom, not the one she'd planned, but she didn't want to go into the bedroom and risk waking the baby—places a bowl of chips on the coffee table, a small dish of sweet pickles, and an ashtray.

"The good news is that here smoking is not prohibited," she proclaims, refreshed. "I was so sick of going to smoke on the sidewalk in all kinds of weather like the whores you see in old French movies."

She lights one; so does Boris.

"Long live delinquency," Marcel says with a snigger.

"And freedom!" Boris says.

Françoise sighs—so as not to cough. Then Marcel begins talking about his children in junior college, Manu in computer science, Cathou in nursing. Françoise stares into space. She'd like to be able to talk about things like that when people ask her about her daughter. But hers had to become infatuated with a good-for-nothing, high on drugs most of the time, and have a child at age nineteen.

≈ The conversation continues like that, more or less. Another bag of chips is opened, a jar of stuffed olives; beer is drunk. Boris has just uncapped his third when Diderot Toussaint shows up, an hour and a half late. Denise springs up.

"You're none too early. I just hope the turkey won't be too dry, with all the time it's been waiting in the oven."

They can finally sit down to dinner. Laure serves the bowls of vegetable soup, Denise brings a basket of bread, the butter that she's just taken out of the refrigerator. The cucumbers and radishes are already on the table.

"Would you mind telling me what actually happened?" Boris asks.

Diderot explains: Boulevard Métropolitain was completely jammed. A truckload of chickens had turned over. The squawking was unreal! What a racket.

"Cages were open. I can't tell you the carnage."

"Please don't," Françoise says with a quaver.

"And my client was getting worked up. Afraid of missing her flight."

"There's a reason they tell you to arrive three hours early," Marcel says.

"As Monsieur de La Fontaine said, there's no point in running."

"Monsieur who?" Denise asks.

"It's a fable," Laure says. "A fable by de La Fontaine. Didn't you ever learn it at school?"

Denise scowls.

"I've learned quite a bit more than you. It's just that I've forgotten some of it."

"There's no point in running, you have to start on time," Diderot says, reciting. "*The Hare and the Tortoise* by Jean de La Fontaine. That said, I think she missed her plane. Completely shattered, the little woman. Her fiancé was waiting for her in the Dominican Republic; she was supposed to get married tomorrow morning. She offered me a one-hundred-dollar tip if I'd get her there on time."

Boris whistles.

Diderot raises his hands in a show of helplessness.

"But how could I? My taxi doesn't have wings."

≈ The plates of turkey are now served. The bowl of cranberry sauce is passed around.

"No wine?" Diderot is surprised.

Françoise starts. She bought it, she assures them, dismayed, a good bottle of Burgundy something, recommended by the employee at the liquor commission. Twenty-three dollars isn't cheap. It's back on the kitchen counter at home.

"I completely forgot; please forgive me. But I can go get it while Lulu sleeps, if you like. It won't take more than fifteen minutes round trip by taxi."

On the verge of tears, she thinks of the thirty dollars that will be added to the price of the bottle.

"Stop with the drama," Denise says. "We can do without. In this heat, red wine goes to the head. I'd just as soon drink beer."

As if to contradict his grandmother, the baby starts crying in the bedroom. Françoise sets down her fork, makes as if she is going to get up, but Laure motions her to stay put.

"Finish eating, Françoise. I'll go take care of him."

"Didn't you say he was good for the night?" Denise says, sighing eloquently.

Diderot suggests adding a drop of rum to his bottle. But Denise doesn't have any rum. They aren't very well going to give him beer.

"I could call Stéph for her to come pick him up," Françoise says.

"Do that."

Gallantly, Diderot hands her his cell phone, as if offering a flower. She dials the number, waits a few instants.

"There's no answer."

"She must have patched things up with her beanpole," Denise says. "And now they're celebrating in the sack."

Françoise casts her a distraught look.

"God forbid!"

Denise bites into a radish.

Dead silence.

"I heard that Potvin lost his driver's license."

"Drunk again, I imagine?" Denise says.

"Went through a red light at the corner of Beaubien and Châteaubriand. Impaired driving."

"Amazing he didn't kill anyone. In any case, you have your vengeance, Diderot."

Last June, Raoul Potvin, by burning Diderot's winning lottery ticket, was responsible for him losing more than two hundred thousand dollars.

He shakes his head.

"Vengeance, perhaps, but as poor as before," he murmurs, wryly.

Françoise picks at her potatoes absent-mindedly.

"You don't seem like yourself, tonight," Marcel says. "Don't you feel well?"

"I don't know. I have a bad feeling."

"Because of your daughter?"

"The heat," Denise says. "It's inhuman, these temperatures. I myself am barely hungry."

"Global warming," Diderot says. "I predict that soon they'll be growing oranges in the Laurentians."

Marcel bursts out laughing. Denise stands abruptly.

"Well, how about moving on to dessert in the meantime?"

She starts to remove their plates, but Boris stops her: he'd take another slice of tourtière. Diderot as well. Marcel is saving his appetite for the sugar pie. He just hopes it will be as good as Marjolaine's.

"Anyway, I asked her for her recipe," Denise says. "You never know, you may even find it better. I replaced her brown sugar with maple sugar."

Françoise is no longer hungry. And Laure hasn't returned. Perhaps she fell asleep with the baby. Dinner drags on in the overheated kitchen.

≈ Almost eleven o'clock. No one wanted coffee. The men have each taken another beer. Denise drank one before the meal, another while eating; now she's sticking to her Diet Coke. She wants to have her mind clear for the game of five hundred. Françoise sips a lukewarm cup of tea. She's having trouble digesting; something didn't go down right. The stuffing, probably. She didn't even eat dessert, or any tourtière, either. Yes, it must be the stuffing. She only took a bit, but it's sitting on her chest. It's as if Denise—or was it Laure? Who made it?—spilled her bowl of savoury into it. The salt shaker as well. Everything was too salty. Françoise never adds salt; it's bad for the arteries. Too rich a meal and too salty. She takes small sips of her tea.

41

They've pushed away the furniture in the living room, set up a table and folding chairs. Françoise, Denise, Boris, and Marcel will play first. Laure and Diderot will face the winners; they await their turn, Diderot on the olive-green couch, Laure pacing, Lulu—finally calmed down—in her arms.

"Now, let's move on to serious things," Boris says.

Denise deals out the cards.

"Eight of hearts," Marcel says.

Boris passes, as do Françoise and Denise. Marcel grabs the kitty. Then Boris puts down the seven of clubs on Marcel's white joker.

"Oh! You don't have a heart."

Denise giggles.

"Everyone knows that."

Three other tricks are won in silence. On the radio, the program *Romantic Cities* ends with *Never on Sunday*. Marcel thinks of Marjolaine on her ship. He knows the cruise itinerary by heart, knows that now they're in Athens, and that she'll spend the entire day there tomorrow. Then the news report begins. A heat record in Montreal; another record forecast for tomorrow. The Minister of Health has resigned.

"What's come over you, Françoise?" Marcel shouts, incensed. "My king of spades was high card, and you have just trumped me. Your jack of diamonds is trump, in case you didn't know."

Denise takes the four tricks face down on the table, in front of Françoise.

"I thought so as well. You didn't follow suit when he played the ace of hearts."

"Excuse me," Françoise says, stammering and on the verge of tears. "Tonight my head's not really in the game."

Laure is afraid that the game will end once more with quarreling. In tragedy, like that fateful evening when Doris passed away in the washroom at the End of the World.

"I can take her place," she says. "She can play later with Diderot."

But Diderot is not in agreement. Françoise promises to concentrate.

"It must be a long time since I've played five hundred."

"It shows," Denise says.

Boris says: "In any case, one thing is certain: you're not the same calibre as your sister."

He remembers their victories: they won at least two times out of three, and not always because they were lucky. In their case, strategy was the keyword.

In Europe, the crisis is still raging, continues the news broadcaster. The credit agency has just lowered Italy's rating by half a point; Greece and Spain are on the verge of disaster. Hurricane Margot has claimed fifty-three victims on the American coast. In Florida, a red alert has been issued; thousands of people have been evacuated. Closer to home, a domestic drama on Boulevard Pie-IX, Montreal's fifteenth murder of the year. The victim, whose identity has not yet been revealed, is a young woman in her early twenties, stabbed, it appears, by her spouse who fled. A neighbour alerted the authorities.

Françoise lets out a strangled cry, drops her hand. Cards fall to the floor. Marcel leans over to pick them up, then shakes his head.

"It's you who had the queen. Frankly, my dear, you're playing terribly."

He takes the others as witnesses.

"How can you win with a partner like that? Might as well play alone," he says, exasperated, brandishing the incriminating queen of hearts.

But Françoise seems petrified. Her lips begin to tremble.

"What's going on?" Denise exclaims. "Are you ill?"

"Sté ..."

She breaks off with a kind of gasp. The others look at her, not understanding.

"Stéphanie."

"What, Stéphanie?"

Tears now fill Françoise's eyes, roll down her cheeks. Her shoulders shake.

"The vi ... victim on Pie-IX ... it's her, it's Stéphanie," she manages to stammer between two sobs.

"What are you talking about?"

"The domestic drama in the neighbourhood," Diderot explains. "They just announced it on the radio. But they said that the victim has not yet been identified."

"Well, you see," Denise says in a tone meant to be reassuring. "You're upsetting yourself for nothing."

"Denise is right," Marcel says. "We don't yet know the name ..."

But Françoise repeats that it's Stéphanie.

"I knew it," she says, moaning. "I knew all evening that something terrifying was happening. A mother knows those things ... That's why she didn't answer the phone."

They are now listening closely, hoping for some snatch of information, but the newscaster has moved on to the elections taking place next week in the Congo. Françoise continues to moan.

"It's her; I feel it. It had to end like that. He always scared me, her beanpole. A druggie, and violent. More than once he threatened to ... to settle the score with her ... finish her off. She told me. I've seen her bruises."

"Come on. There are hundreds of young women on Boulevard Pie-IX. It's not necessarily your daughter."

"I should have stayed with her. It wouldn't have happened. You never should have invited me. I didn't want to come. It's too hot to eat turkey, and now I feel sick. And I hate playing cards. There's always a drama during your damned games of five hundred."

"Don't blame us now," Denise says.

They all begin to talk at once.

"Perhaps she's just injured."

"It's true, no one said she was dead."

"If it's her."

"*Victim* is the word they used."

"And usually when they use that word ..."

"They said murder. Montreal's fifteenth murder of the year."

"Call her."

But Françoise is transfixed to her chair, unable to get up to go to the landline, and it's Boris' turn to hand his cell phone to her.

"Yes, call her. That way you'll find out."

There is still no answer, but Françoise can't bring herself to stop hoping, the telephone glued to her ear. Denise takes it out of her hands and gives it back to Boris.

"I told you, the baby isn't there, so they're making the most of it," she says. "Now they're—"

"Stop," Marcel says. "Stop, Denise, that's enough."

Everyone falls silent. As if they too suddenly had the same certainty, as if they knew that the young woman stabbed, the victim, was Stéphanie.

His head on Laure's shoulder, Lulu has finally fallen asleep.

3

The *End of the World,* Late Morning

They all have a telephone in hand,
ready for a selfie.
The Minister of Health has resigned ...

COMINGS AND GOINGS on the deck, the hum of conversation, a laugh bursting forth, and the sea so blue. A guy paces back and forth, concentrating hard: two serious men play chess. They're always playing, and when they're not playing, they discuss in their language topics that do not seem light. It's rather strange to go on a cruise and spend so much time in front of a chess board. Béatrice thinks they are practicing for a tournament; she must be right. Marjolaine has never seen them disembark at the ports of call. She herself hasn't missed any. She doesn't see the British. There are four of them: a novelist—she gave one of her books, signed, to John Paradis; her brother, a rather attractive man in his fifties; a beautiful jet-black woman; and a whippersnapper with thinning hair. It is not teatime, however. The author and the scrawny fellow take it at four o'clock every afternoon—served to them with cucumber sandwiches, a strange idea. A small cute blond couple, her eyes green, his blue, on honeymoon, looking hungrily at one another. Another couple, not so cute, eccentric, let us say, whose appearance clashes with that of the other passengers, lean against the ship's rail. Smiling widely, with their digital cameras or their smartphones, Japanese people photograph everything they see: the waves, the decks, the deck chairs, the passengers. And, when they're on land, they photograph the islanders, the monuments, the ruins, the cypresses and lemon trees, the seagulls and the fishing nets. The pink horizon at dusk, the moon quivering on the sea. Even the dishes served to them in the dining room. They are not the only ones; everyone does that. Except Marjolaine: she prefers postcards, buys one at each port of call in addition to souvenirs, bracelets, T-shirts, magnets, and lighters that she'll give to friends and family. An American woman, silent and unsociable, always in black. A widow, perhaps? On a deck chair a bit farther away, a girl with blue hair taps on her cell phone. A singer. French and very popular, apparently. Zoé, Chloé, a name like that. No, Daphné, that's it. She is travelling with her sister and their mother. Marjolaine doesn't know her. Or maybe she does. At the End of the World, she heard millions of songs on the radio without always knowing who was singing. In any case, they'll be impressed, in Montreal, maybe even a bit jealous when they find out she travelled with a well-known singer and two chess champions.

As for the crew, they come mainly from Eastern Europe, from the former Soviet bloc. Except for the officers who are Italian or French.

≈ John Paradis now approaches and sits down on the deck chair next to Marjolaine. Besides him and Béatrice, other Quebecers are on board the ship. She noticed Kim Dupont, the boss' daughter, who cleans cabins. Kim doesn't seem to know that she's been let go; she'd already left when the event occurred. She asked her if she found the cuisine on the ship inspiring, if they were going to savour new dishes at "the other End of the World." Marjolaine merely nodded her head, not really answering, putting on a forced smile. Why feel worse? There are other Quebecers she doesn't know. A young poet, for example, who washes dishes and cleans vegetables in the ship's galley. And then that sad trio—she knows why. The couple lost their daughter in Florida last winter. She recognizes the father, saw him on TV a few times, on the news and in those programs where they interview all kinds of people who are suffering. As if that weren't enough, his other daughter, an adopted Chinese girl, falsely accused him of incest on a reality TV show. Afterwards she refuted it, but the harm was done. Oh, now that she thinks of it, the disloyal daughter was called Daphné, like the singer. There is no justice; misfortune strikes some people more than others. These people don't mix with the other passengers; it's understandable that they want to protect their sorrow—can one protect it? The third must be a family member, a brother or cousin of one or the other. Most probably a brother. His face looks familiar; she's already seen him, but doesn't know where; in the restaurant perhaps, or on the street if he lives in her neighbourhood. They must be inconsolable, devastated. Marjolaine would be. She'd never have left on a cruise if her daughter had disappeared. But she refuses to judge them.

"You look sorrowful, this morning, Marjolaine. A problem?"

She shakes her head. No. No, I'm okay."

"Are you sad because the journey's ending?"

"No. I'm not sad. Maybe a little. I don't know."

She sighs.

"It's because of the book, I think, the one Béatrice gave me. The history of Christopher Columbus. I thought that ... I mean, I didn't think he was ..."

"He was what?"

"So cruel."

John Paradis adopts a surprised expression. Cruel? Christopher Columbus? No, it was certainly not cruelty that made him famous.

"Before, I admired him," Marjolaine says.

"Cruel, no, Marjolaine: that's not what I'd say about him. At least no crueller than the others. The times were cruel. And you were right to admire him. He was a great man. A dreamer, yes, but humanity needs dreamers to advance. Without dreamers, we wouldn't be what we are."

And that would perhaps be preferable, she thinks. But she keeps the thought to herself.

They, since the second day, have agreed to call each other by their first names. It is he who suggested it. On a ship, he said, especially on a ship like the *End of the World*, of human dimensions, if, however, "human" is the right word—only two hundred passengers, sixty crew—a human ship and not a floating city, one of those monsters that travel and pollute the planet's oceans shamelessly, it's a bit as if they temporarily made up a large family. A large family—not really, in the end, observed Marjolaine. Each one only seeing their fellow citizens: the Arabs eat together, the Japanese men dance with Japanese women, the Americans too. That is people from the

United States; John Paradis claims that is the way to refer to them; he corrects her each time, saying they are imperialists, it is not true that their country is called America —we are Americans from the North Pole to Tierra del Fuego. But Marjolaine had nothing against calling each other by their first names, even if it seemed strange to address a university professor like that.

"I was very naïve, I imagine," she murmurs. "I didn't ask myself enough questions."

He remains silent for a moment, then:

"Naiveté is part of your charm, Marjolaine."

Her charm? No one, not even Marcel, has ever said she had any. Or if he said so to her, it was a long time ago.

"He was Jewish, apparently," she says, dreamily.

"On his mother's side."

"In my book, they say that it was his father's family. That they had to flee Spain because of persecution. Because in that time as well they persecuted Jews."

John Paradis says that it's simple: they haven't read the same book.

"Most historians claim he was Italian. But others think he was French, or Spanish, Maltese, Basque, Portuguese. They claim he was born in Genoa. I've seen the supposed ruins of his birth house in Corsica, in Calvi. He himself never revealed where he came from."

She wonders why there are all these mysteries. Someone tells us something, we think it's true. Someone else comes along and tells something else. In the end, you no longer know who's telling the truth. History is not an exact science, as John Paradis told her. In the beginning, we descended from Adam and Eve completely naked in the earthly paradise. Now, our ancestors are a couple of monkeys. For her, all these contradictions are destabilizing. All the same, without really believing it, she finds it nicer with Adam and Even than a couple of orangutans. When she said that in front of her children, they rolled their eyes to the sky, replied that evolution has been proven since Darwin and she'd be better off giving up her reactionary theories.

"Apparently he cut off the noses or ears of Indians," she says, "the Indigenous, I mean. First Nations, if that's how they call them in the Caribbean. For nothing, just out of cruelty. Just for stealing a shirt, sometimes."

"Do you really think the Indigenous were any gentler to them? Think of human sacrifice."

"He sent thousands to Spain, as slaves. The holds full. His men raped the girls. Some arrived there pregnant. Do you think they acknowledged their children?"

John Paradise shakes his head.

"At least he discovered America," she says finally, a tad reluctantly.

But John Paradis says that they're not even sure that he discovered it. One of his sailors may have been captured by a Turkish pirate. According to him, Columbus read a book, dating from the time of Alexander the Great, in which the author spoke of a continent beyond the Ocean Sea, or the Mare Nostrum, depending on the translation. He followed the directions and that's how he arrived in the Caribbean. Other researchers believe that the Phoenicians already knew the way. Not to mention the Vikings"

"Stop John, you're making me dizzy."

It's true: first, we don't know where he was born.

Whether he was Jewish or Christian, Spanish or Italian. And now we're not even sure that he discovered America. Everything depends upon the book you read? News to her.

"And others think that ten thousand years ago in America there existed a very advanced civilization that was familiar with iron and knew how to write. Truth does not exist. It advances and retreats. It's a concept, a dream. Every time someone thinks they've found it someone comes along and finds the opposite. And they all have proof."

Marjolaine says nothing. Then: "There were cannibals. In Cuba. At least, if it's true. I thought it was just in Africa."

John Paradis shrugs his shoulders, says that there were cannibals everywhere at all times.

"Not anymore," Marjolaine says.

"And Hannibal Lecter?"

"Yes, but that's in a movie. I couldn't watch it to the end. In any case, he's a character: he never existed."

"Perhaps not him. But there have been others. Everywhere, I insist. Look, in China, for example, right in the middle of the twentieth century, during the famines that followed the Great Leap Forward." And then, seeing her puzzled look: "The Cultural Revolution, Mao Zedong."

"Sometimes I have the impression that you and Béatrice take me for a retard."

"Not on your life! Quite the opposite. It's true, I do repeat things, clarify them, but there you go, I taught my whole life. These are an old professor's quirks."

He really does look sorry.

"More than anything, I don't want to hurt you."

"Mmmmm ..."

"All in all, our history is rather horrible: you are right, Marjolaine. With its cannibals, its stakes, its torture. But it is ours. Good and evil exist side by side."

She thinks he has spoken well, even if it's far from reassuring.

"And there are wonderful moments, fortunately. Our cruise, for example," he says. "Don't tell me otherwise."

≈ Raised voices now. The weird couple is having an animated discussion. She, a redhead (but with black roots); at least five or six months pregnant, Marjolaine has assessed, perhaps even with twins, and painfully thin with a belly that sticks out like a balloon between her sharp hips. And always so tackily decked out: today in a canary-yellow minidress far too clinging for her condition—featuring a tiger or tigress baring its teeth—tights with a blue and red diamond pattern, worn pink ballet shoes on her feet. Anything to be noticed. Marjolaine has even seen her strut around in a bikini, and more than once, at the pool. And she smokes like a chimney. He, with a shaved head, a ring piercing his right eyebrow, another in his left ear, impressive biceps featuring tattoos of disturbing two-headed creatures with wings and horns, and esoteric inscriptions. The girl also has a black feline tattooed on her shoulder. Most of the time, they seem to be arguing in Italian, or Spanish—a Latin language, in any case. John Paradis says they go from one to the other. "He is Argentine, I would say, due to the accent. The girl is unquestionably Italian." One minute they're quarrelling, the next they're in each other's arms. Marjolaine even surprised them the other day in the small lounge, the girl's hand placed on the guy's sex, quite obviously erect, while he was groping her breasts. While everyone could see them — Marjolaine saw them clearly. The guy actually gave her a lewd wink. She left without further ado. Béatrice and John Paradis laughed hard when she told them about the incident. For her, that is called lacking class. The wink, especially.

So he speaks in Spanish and she in Italian. Because John Paradis always seems to know everything. Hidden behind a newspaper or a serious magazine that he buys at the ports of call, his nose in a book or tapping away on the screen of his tablet, he still always seems to be on the lookout. Nothing escapes him. Sometimes he jots down things in a notebook that he takes out of his shirt pocket. He reminds her somewhat of that guy, at the End of the World, always scribbling away in a notebook. Except that one was taciturn. Denise — or Laure? — had nicknamed him the Boogeyman. Polite, however. He never forgot to say "please" in his deep voice when he ordered his lemon tea, "thank you," when they brought it to him. Béatrice would come once a week to join him in the evening.

And then John Paradis, who seemed to speak, or jabber away in and understand a good dozen languages, connects with everyone. Only the American woman in black still resists his attempts to reach out to her. Try as he might, she responded in monosyllables to comments such as *Such a nice day today, isn't it?* Shy? Misanthropic? In mourning? How to know? John says that she resembles Misia, queen of Paris at the Belle Époque, a friend of famous people in their time, writers, painters who did her portrait, musicians who played for her. Marjolaine guesses he would not say no if the opportunity arose. Even with her, he would not say no, she would swear to it. A kind of Don

Juan on the decline who collects conquests everywhere he goes. Not for her. She is faithful to her Marcel, always has been. Well, almost always. She also has a flower in her secret garden: who hasn't? Raoul Potvin, a few years ago, when his wife was so sick and he so desperate—it happened two or three times. Not a flower, all in all, a stinging nettle, a weed scratching the memory. She prefers not to think about it. Because if she thinks about it, something bitter—shame?—rises in her throat.

Be that as it may, she wonders how it would be with JP—she and Béatrice call him JP when they speak of him. She has rarely spent time with such a refined man. Never, to tell the truth. With his short grey beard, his reading glasses: he is rather attractive for his type. He smokes a pipe. And it's incredible all the man knows: you'd think he'd read every book. True, he taught literature. He spent the week telling her stories: gods who consumed their children, others who transformed themselves into bulls or swans or had their livers pecked away at for eternity. There was even a king, Xerxes, who one day had the Aegean Sea whipped to punish it for breaking a bridge. And Aegeus was the name of another king who threw himself into the water when he believed his son was dead. In one week, she feels as if she's learned more than in the forty-some years of her life.

He takes his tablet out of his canvas bag.

"Want news of back home?"

He receives his daily newspaper on the Web. Otherwise, he follows the news, also on the Web. A funny idea, to leave home and act as if you were still there. He calls that the gift of being … ubi something. Marjolaine forgets what. He says that it's like being everywhere at once.

She nods her head.

"So you'll be conversant."

"Conversant?"

"In the know. If you don't want to land the day after tomorrow completely disconnected."

This news of back home is not something she really wants.

In two days she'll be there and that's soon enough. He touches the screen and whistles softly.

"Thirty-six degrees in the shade in Montreal. That's the forecast for today."

Unheard of for late September.

Oh well, there you go, she thinks, annoyed. *Louison and her gang of friends will be able to fill themselves with those kuski things all the way to the sidewalk.*

"Well what do you know? Masson has resigned. That was to be expected."

She furrows her brow.

"Jules Masson, the Minister of Health. You know, after the tainted meat scandal in the nursing homes. The media have been talking only about that for a month. People demonstrated in front of the Ministry. He couldn't do otherwise even though he wasn't really responsible."

Marjolaine sighs. Since the economic crisis, it's as if people have lost all sense of morality. However, it is not the first crisis or the last, assuredly, that humanity has gone or will go through. So it has it learned nothing from its past errors? Apparently not, it learns nothing, ever. God knows what awaits us when our turn comes to depend on the government.

"They've just arrested the person responsible for the attack in Paris," he says in the same indulgent tone. "At

Harry's Bar, last June, remember? And you know what? It was a close call for me; I was there a few days before it happened. I spoke with someone called Block, Henry or Andy, a drama critic for a New York magazine, a stout guy—very funny, deadpan sense of humour, outrageous. Unfortunately, he wasn't so lucky … They found the young Laframboise girl. At least what remains of her. You know, the teenager who disappeared in Florida last winter."

Marjolaine emits a muffled cry.

"I knew it!"

John Paradis looks up. She says that things always end like that when children disappear. Almost always. Particularly when it's been so long. And the parents, on the ship. Perhaps they hadn't any more hope either, that's why, why they left on a trip, she ends before making a kind of botched sign of the cross.

"Are you a believer, Marjolaine?" he asks, surprised.

She shrugs her shoulders.

"Well, no," she says, vaguely ashamed.

Then: "I don't really know. It's as if I don't know what to believe."

"Agnostic, then."

Always with the big words.

"It's against nature when children go before their parents."

She's thinking of her own, of course.

"And, if the news is all bad, I'll find out about it quickly enough once I'm home."

"Understood. Excuse me. I certainly didn't want to be a killjoy."

He continues to update himself in silence. Then he glances at his watch.

"Come, let's not speak of it anymore; you're right, it's too sad. We should end this cruise in high spirits. Come, let's go in to dinner. Béatrice must be waiting for us. And you know she doesn't like that."

4

Domestic Drama on the Other Side of the Cardboard Wall

He wants to see Mayerling, where
an archduke died.
Closer to home, a domestic drama on
Boulevard Pie-IX ...

Rudolf suddenly feels Mary's desire throbbing
beneath his fingers ... At present, the girl is now
sure: her love is shared: the heart of the
handsome unhappy archduke beats in rhythm
with her own in mutual passion.

GINETTE SHRUGS HER shoulders. What rubbish, really. She marks the page with a bookmark, a postcard, rather, that shows three palm trees standing like sentinels in front of a turquoise sea, and places the book on the coffee table, letting her mind wander.

When it comes to embellishing reality, you can always count on novels. There, for example. A few words and the entire situation is evoked. Desire throbbing. You feel it. No need for erotic descriptions with the names of organs and orifices, words that are never pretty. Besides, Ginette thinks, it's far more erotic without the descriptions—otherwise, it's pornography. Light touching, intent looks, the breath of the other on the skin, the breath

60

of passion. And desire that suddenly throbs. Almost painful, but at the same time so sweet, voluptuous, at the core.

That, of course, is in novels. In real life, in hers at least, it's different.

Besides, she knows how the story ends. Badly, of course, in death; isn't that how stories always end? But she's not sure that things happened so romantically, with mutual passion, hearts throbbing in unison, all that. Just words to make people dream. This is the third book she's read on the topic—not to mention the movie and the TV series—and all contradict one another. Things must have happened like that in real life.

In the movie—an old French movie that she recently saw again on TV early in the summer—the lovers killed themselves; their love was impossible. They could not resign themselves to live without one another. Ginette couldn't help but shed a few tears—people have always reproached her for being too sensitive; Robert, especially, made fun of what he called her "sentimentality," shrugging his shoulders when she burst into tears at the end of a novel or a film. He no longer wanted go to movies with her. But in the first book, the biography of the archduke, it was about an assassination for political motives that she didn't really understand. The Hungarian plot with all kinds of characters and names of unpronounceable places. Here, no question of an impossible love: Mary was a kind of a ... how do they say it? Collateral victim, that's it. In the TV series, Rudolf killed Mary before putting a bullet through his head, but not at all because he was madly in love with the innocent young thing—she was seventeen. Out of despair. All his plans for reform fell through and, struck with an incurable—venereal—

61

disease, he suffered too much. The second book offered another version of the facts. Rudolf learned that his pregnant mistress was also his half-sister: his father the Emperor had a liaison with Baroness Vetsera, Mary's mother, eighteen years earlier. He ordered him to break it off. Death, a double suicide, was the only way out for the doomed lovers. She also read the biography of Rudolf's mother, the enigmatic Sissi. This time, the fickle prince wanted to leave Mary, who had become a nuisance. He coveted someone else; the spurned woman poisoned him with potassium cyanide then killed herself with Rudolf's revolver. All those hypotheses: you could get lost. The past is full of mysteries and lies. In the end, historians contradict one another; biographies are not reliable. It's the same today. For do we really know who killed John Kennedy and why? Some think it was a visionary; others blame the FBI or the CIA. Some implicate Marilyn Monroe. The faithless one was dead because of her or the opposite was true: she died because of him. In her case, people vacillate equally between murder and suicide, and in the end, everyone believes what they want.

The book she's reading is entitled *Mayerling or The Unresolved Enigma*, a historical novel—with undeniable sentimental undertones—by Juliette Evangelic, now her favourite author. Three hundred and sixty-six pages. She borrowed it yesterday from the library and is on page 140. It will keep her busy for the rest of the day, a good part of the evening, and she'll finish it tomorrow.

Three o'clock. Oppressive heat. During a heatwave, drinking a lot is recommended, and not moving around too much. She's made a pitcher of iced tea.

She resumes reading. A first meeting takes place between the two characters, a walk in the Prater, a Viennese park. For Mary, it's love at first sight: she records it in her diary when she returns home. For him, it's less clear. A few days pass; messages are exchanged through willing servants. A date is made. She has just arrived at the palace; a valet leads her to the prince's private apartments. A tamed raven, Rudolf's mascot, greets her with the beating of black wings. She spots a human skull on the desk. A bad omen: she should run away. But already her desire is throbbing.

Oh, there's the baby next door—his name is Lulu, go figure out why, to her ears it sounds more like a cat's name—who is starting to shout himself hoarse. It's seldom that he can't be heard screaming at the top of his lungs: the poor child must be suffering from colic. Daphné was like that: probably she had been malnourished in her Chinese orphanage. They say there was melamine in the infant formula. No, she's mixed up; that scandal is more recent. Still, who knows what they gave those babies? Or Lulu is anxious: some little babies suffer from anxiety as well, apparently, and this one has lots of reasons to be. His parents spend their time shouting insults at one another, sometimes suspicious noises can be heard. When Ginette meets them on the stairs, they don't even have the common courtesy to greet her. As for apologizing for the disturbances and sleepless nights they put her through, forget it. It obviously never occurred to them. Badly brought up: that's the least one can say.

"Damned idiot!"

"You're the idiot! You make me sick! Why don't you go hang out with your damned dancers?"

"Good idea!"

That's it, they're at it again. They shout so loudly that Ginette doesn't miss a word. It's true the walls are made of cardboard here; you always know who has a cold, what program the neighbours are watching. But today those two seem to be shouting more loudly than usual. Or it's because the windows are open. In any case, it's enlightening. It's about money, of course, the money he burned in strip clubs and now the refrigerator is empty: nothing left to eat except for Lulu's cereal. The welfare cheque won't arrive for ten days, and for a change she'll have to go beg for cans at Moisson Montréal, and appeal to her mother for charity, who'll sigh and end up taking out a miserable twenty-dollar bill from her wallet, barely enough to pay for the baby's milk. Voices are raised again, and Ginette would rather not hear the insults they shout at one another. Incredible, the words people find when they want to humiliate and wound others.

"Sometimes I wonder why don't you drop dead when you're driving around stoned out of your mind in that fucking car!"

Why don't you drop dead? Can a person really say that, even blinded by anger? She isn't wrong, though, Ginette must admit. She even remembers thinking it herself a few times, at night, mostly, when Robert left her for another woman. If only you'd die. When he was late coming home, in the middle of the night, she was always afraid he'd be dead, the victim of a hit-and-run, a stray bullet. When he left she began hoping the stray bullet would hit him right in the heart and he'd be truly dead. When she is humiliated, scorned, a woman thinks those things.

And the baby, shouting at the top of its lungs. Will

they kill one another? Ginette has seen, and not only once, the girl go out in the rain with dark glasses. She was hiding a black eye, it was obvious. Shouldn't she call the police? Perhaps the child is in danger. She hesitates. What should a person do in such cases? Surely the police cannot intervene each time there's a domestic dispute. And it might likely inflame things even more. Because afterwards, if her neighbour learns she reported him, he could attack her, and then what. No one knows what that kind of man is capable of. Of the worst, probably.

The door slams so violently that a picture in Ginette's living room falls to the floor. In a way, so much the better. She should have thrown it in the garbage a long time ago. One of those naïve paintings with flowers and birds in garish colours that young men—girls too—sell on the beaches in the Dominican Republic. A bad memory of Cabarete. When a dream, a stupid dream, turned into a nightmare, a sordid nightmare. A guy, far too young for her in any case, came on to her by the water: she thought she was in the middle of a romantic novel. In the end, he vanished, stealing her wallet while she slept. A real cliché. He told her one thing and another, whispered sweet words with his accent, and she, like an imbecile … Had she seen such a melodrama on TV, she wouldn't have shed a tear.

It was his cousin Raúl who did the naïve paintings.

The baby is still crying. How to read with that racket? Impossible to concentrate. So despite the overwhelming heat, "extreme" as they call it on the radio, and despite the wise advice they keep repeating since this morning, she grabs her purse. She's going out, will get some air. If there is any.

≈ During her walk, she practically collides with a guy in black, a rather handsome man in his own way — tall, slim, hair tied back on the neck, a three-day beard — who mumbles a few incomprehensible words and continues on his way. Odd, she hadn't seen him coming. Where had he come from? She must have been lost in her thoughts. Reaching home, bathed in sweat, out of breath, she runs into the grandmother coming out with Lulu in her stroller. She checks her watch: four thirty.

She enters her place, giving a sigh of relief. Silence, finally, silence reigns in the house. Silence is a blessing. Providing the grandma keeps him for the night, she thinks. But she doesn't kid herself. In a few hours, the old lady will bring him back and farewell tranquility. She starts. The old lady? What got into her to think that word, "old lady?" They were both about the same age. And her daughter, the hysterical one next door, the age of her own daughter, Daphné.

Her adopted daughter, in fact, who hasn't been in touch. A terse postcard from Paradise Island, the one with three coconut trees, last May, to say she was still alive, she was well. Since then, nothing. She must still be there, as far as Ginette knows. What is she doing there? A mystery. She has trouble containing her impatience. She's hiding, of course, after the scandal she provoked when she appeared on the program. *Seventh Heaven*, a reality TV show. Ginette has not seen it; reality TV doesn't interest her. It's enough to endure reality all day long and not be faced with it again in the evening when you turn on the TV. In any case, how could she have known that Daphné would be on it? No one ever tells her anything.

While she didn't see it, she heard about it. For some time, they spoke only of that. Letters from readers in the newspapers, talk lines on the radio. It was in March; the media must have had nothing juicier to explore just then. A girl falsely accused her adoptive father of sexually abusing her as a child. She lied, and after all the accusations in recent months, that was what was so shocking. Ginette couldn't get over it when she finally understood what it was about—gossipy Denise of course took pleasure in calling her to fill her in. Robert Laframboise, her ex-husband, and their daughter Daphné, the baby they had gone to fetch in China. And the scandal broke—the bomb burst—barely a few months after the disappearance of Robert's other daughter, Fanny, in Florida, around Christmas. In quick succession. Enough to shatter a man, even a proud and strong one like him.

Journalists—of scandal sheets—managed to track her down—the mother of the pariah, in her three and a half, Boulevard Pie-IX, and ask her to comment. She of course denied everything. But the shame, afterwards, the fear of being recognized in the neighbourhood.

When she thinks of Robert's fate, even though he deserved it—maybe it's shocking, but she feels avenged: he got his own, life saw to that—when she thinks about it, she almost manages to find hers enviable, that's for sure. Bearable, at least. While other people's misfortune never makes us happy, in this case it at least had the advantage of bringing her out of her depression. She who had been despondent since her own adventure, or misadventure, in the Dominican Republic basically no longer thinks of it anymore since the events.

Why did Daphné do it? What got into her? Ginette has asked herself the question for months without understanding. There is no explanation. Daphné wanted to win, obviously. She always spoke of returning to China, as if life were better there. The program was a kind of contest where candidates were eliminated one by one. The one who remained, the victor, received a tidy sum: one hundred thousand dollars, tax free. From what she understood, it was to amaze and above all seduce the TV audience who, at the end, would vote for their favourite. Amaze, seduce, and move them, most of all. But that is not enough to explain the inexplicable. She could have moved them by telling them something else, no matter what, like the others did. It wasn't necessary to slander. Daphné had always been hard-hearted, if she even had a heart, which Ginette sometimes doubts. In any case, it was not she who won. All that for nothing. Except for the trip to Paradise Island—a consolation prize—where she must still be hiding out. Well, so much the better for Daphné if she found a paradise, because here is anything but.

Unless she was still mad at Robert for the separation, hadn't been able to forgive him for being abandoned a second time. At the time, however, she had not reacted. But she'd always been secretive, closed. An oyster—useless to go looking for a pearl. You never knew what she was thinking, feeling, if she felt anything at all. Except for the desire to leave for China.

What if it was true, Ginette wondered once more. Anything can be, after all, the unthinkable as well, too often. You have only to watch the news with the terrorist attacks in the world, serial killers roaming around, and not only in the United States. What if it had really happened like that? She searched her memory looking for clues, but found nothing. Did he linger too long when he tucked her into bed? She didn't think so. Besides, most of the time it was she who tucked her in. And when he took her for rides in the car? Were there inappropriate gestures, misconduct, as they say nowadays? Daphné never spoke of it, but do you confide everything to your mother, even—and especially—the adoptive one? The most important thing, the unmentionable, you keep to yourself: it's well known. There are always some grey areas that remain: she read that sentence somewhere, she forgets where. Some call it a secret garden. A garden of thistles, that's for sure, or even cacti, in the case of Daphné.

We don't understand other people. Most of the time their motives escape us. Even when we thought we loved them, they remain strangers.

Yet, I loved you, both of you, she repeated, trying to convince herself. We loved one another. And if that love in no way resembles what she saw in movies or read in books, she did everything she could, everything I could, she says. For her as well as for him. Everything I could. And, in a way, it's true.

In books, everything is explained: we know why he or she did what they did. Even Hannibal, in *The Silence of the Lambs*, experienced tragedy in his childhood. There is always a reason and the author knows it. The reader is reassured.

≈ Moving: that thought obsesses her. She can't bear this neighbourhood anymore, or life in this dump. She may have decorated it to her taste, with her meagre means, on

a shoestring budget, as they say, but it's still a dump—
let's not mince words. Living in such close quarters,
neighbours coughing and shouting: she can no longer
stand it. She's thinking about one of those residences for
independent seniors, for instance. They are advertised on
TV. You see folks there, not all that old, in the end—you
have to be at least fifty—playing cards in rooms with
sunshine flooding in, sitting in swings in a flowered garden, a book or piece of knitting in their lap, or being
served a meal by attendants who always seem to be smiling. A fine way to end one's life. In dignity.

In three years she'll be in her fifties, it's true. She's
independent, that's true too, but retired from what? She
never worked. And those residences are not cheap, far
from it. To live there, you need money. She hasn't any;
and never will have; no inheritance to look forward to
from anyone. Unless she wins the lottery, but she can't
even afford to buy tickets. Robert stopped paying her
alimony since Daphné left. Selfish and stingy, with no
consideration for the years of youth she sacrificed for
him. She lives—survives, rather—on her meagre welfare
cheque, as do most of the tenants in the building with the
cardboard walls. In about twenty years, it will be the old
age pension. So it's pointless to dream. She'll end her life
in a nursing home, without dignity, eating tainted meat.
They talked about it on the news: the Minister of Health
even had to resign. She turned off the radio after learning that.

Perhaps she dreamed her life. That's what her psychologist told her—she sees her once a month at the local
community service centre. Novels, movies too, have helped
her. And they harmed her; she knows that now. She lived

vicariously, hundreds of lives, except her own, because her own she did not choose. She would be Anne Boleyn, Cleopatra, or Sissi, and if their destiny was tragic, at least it was a destiny. Oh! To advance slowly, nobly, to offer the executioner her slender neck, collapse elegantly beneath a thrusted dagger, an anarchist's bullet. She could have been called Sophie Alexandrovna, been secretly in love with a Nicholas Federovitch with smouldering eyes, member of a group of revolutionaries who wanted to assassinate the czar, place a bomb beneath his coach; she would have convinced him to give up his plan. Destiny, our own, that of the world — why should we accept it? We can change it: you just have to have imagination.

It's over. The romance novels, the *True Emotions* collection, Hope Spencer and the others; she has given them up since the humiliating episode in Cabarete. She only reads historical novels now. Strange, when you think about it, all those little girls who disguised themselves as princesses, awaiting Prince Charming as she herself awaited him for too long. You only have to be a little interested in history to understand that princesses had far from easy lives. Married, sold, to say the word, sometimes from birth, to strangers, often ugly or deformed, afflicted with the worst defects, who cheated on them, ridiculed them, sent them off to foreign courts, obliged to follow strict protocols, always closely watched, without a moment's freedom. And the tragedy when they were sterile or thought to be, when they had the misfortune to bring a daughter into the world. As if they were responsible for the child's gender. As if it were shameful to give birth to a daughter. They were there only to procreate, to ensure the survival of the dynasty. That happened to Rudolf's legitimate wife, a rather drab Belgian princess called Stéphanie. And they try to make us believe that they all lived in a fairy tale.

In any case, if she believes what she has read, that prince was anything but charming. She has seen his photos—in the old days, photos were not altered; they didn't lie like today. Moustached, forbidding, stilted— not her type at all: she wonders what Mary and the others could have seen in him. What's more, he was depraved and cheated on his wife with all women who crossed his path, countesses and prostitutes alike, married or not. He even contaminated the poor Stéphanie: that's why she couldn't have other children, the male heir that everyone awaited.

Oh, now that she thinks about it, the girl next door, who looks nothing like a princess, is also called Stéphanie. A name that must bring misfortune.

But now everything is silent. If it could only last.

She no longer wants to think of her difficulties, or those of Robert, of her neighbours or of disenchanted princesses. She has other plans for the evening. She'll turn on her fan in the living room, read her book, quite peaceful, sitting on her couch, feet on her hassock, listening to music, Viennese waltzes, perhaps, for the local colour, or Charles Aznavour or Joe Dassin. She'll prepare a healthy tray for herself: baby carrots, slices of Lebanese cucumber, berry yogurt, iced tea, three soda crackers, and a chocolate bar. To finish, she could even treat herself to a shot of dark rum: she brought back a bottle from Cabarete that she keeps for special occasions. While there's nothing special to celebrate, she thinks she deserves a bit of sweetness after the furor and the shouting earlier.

Page 160. A work by Richard Wagner, *The Rhinegold*, is being presented at the Vienna Opera. All of high society is attending. The lovers take advantage. They don't have much time, scarcely two hours. What does it matter? *We gave ourselves to one another*, admits the unfortunate Mary in a letter to her piano teacher, a certain Hermine. When it's in a letter, there's no question. The die is cast. It is written black on white on page 167 of the novel.

She chooses three CDs, all three of them Aznavour. She has always loved his voice.

This evening, no TV. She looked at the TV listings: nothing interests her. A TV reality show, *Emotions*, in fact, where people come on to talk about their life, at least the harrowing episodes, and burst into tears in front of the camera. On other channels, an American police show full of psychopaths, a special on the economic crisis, and a documentary entitled "Big Cats," today: the cougar. You always end up seeing them pounce on their prey, a harmless doe or gazelle, devour it still ... quivering, that's it. Quivering. Ginette wonders: do you have an orgasm when you die?

≈ "I told you never to set foot in here again!"

"I live here! I'll leave when I want!"

"You don't even pay rent!"

Well, well. The neighbour has returned. It was too good to last. Ginette turns up the volume on the CD player, tries to concentrate again on her reading.

"Big fat dirty cow! Will you shut up!"

Fat? He's exaggerating. A bit plump, perhaps, rolls of fat here and there. The poor woman doesn't eat properly, that's why. Ginette has seen her, far too often, come out of the McDonald's a little down the road, her baby in her arms.

Now it's as if Aznavour is wailing ... wailing that Venice is sad. All cities are when love is dead. And if they're not yet dead next door, they're certainly on their way.

Aznavour is wailing, but the neighbours are wailing even more loudly. Ginette hears other noises. Hitting? He's beating her, she is certain; he's hitting her while she, next door, remains there doing nothing, paralyzed, terrorized.

Now, footsteps on the staircase. He didn't slam the door, this time. She hears the car, a jalopy start: the corner is turned at top speed. The silence now reigning in the apartment next door does not bode well.

"My God," Ginette murmurs. "Say it isn't so."

She imagines her neighbour, still young, far too young to die—she is Daphné's age, their two faces become superimposed and confused in the space of a moment—she imagines her lying, curled up in a pool of blood. In the building, no reaction: everyone continues to go about their business. As if nothing had happened. But that couple quarrels all the time: people are used to it. Ginette would like to go investigate, but doesn't dare. He could return. She doesn't dare.

She reaches for the telephone, dials 911. Addressing a God she is not sure she believes in, she repeats her litany:

"Say it isn't so. Say I'm mistaken. Say it isn't so ..."

5

The *End of the World*, Lunch Hour

What does it matter, in the end, if these stories were true or not?

... two serious men play chess.

A dreamer, yes, but humanity needs dreamers to advance.

FOR THE MOMENT, they are alone in the ship's restaurant. First come, first served, and Béatrice doesn't like waiting. John and Marjolaine have agreed to say nothing about Fanny Laframboise. Talking about it won't change anything, and will only make their last lunch aboard the *End of the World* sad. Besides, Béatrice certainly doesn't know about it. She adamantly refuses to hear news from home when she's on vacation — on that point, she is even more adamant than Marjolaine.

Marjolaine wonders how long the parents have known. Were they telephoned? Sent a message? Or perhaps they discovered it on the Internet like everyone? She discussed it with John; he thinks they were informed before the news was broadcast. She wonders if they'll come eat. Surely not, no. They won't be able to. In any case, in their situation she wouldn't be able to swallow a thing. Perhaps a helicopter will come for them? Is it possible that they'll still have to wait two interminable days before going to retrieve or identify their child's body? Will it even be identifiable? Nevertheless, she watches the door, hoping not to see them enter. Because what do you do in cases like that? Do you rush to the mother, take her in your arms? What do you say? My condolences? My sympathies?

She ordered a Greek salad. She's never very hungry at lunch. Béatrice too, but as an appetizer, followed by a dish of pasta—with her chubbiness, she's going too far, Marjolaine notes with regret, especially since she's going to order dessert, perhaps two, chocolate things always topped with whipped cream—and John Paradis, steak tartare: he orders that half the time. Raw meat, topped with an egg yolk. It revolts her to see him eat that. At the End of the World, her own End of the World, no one would ever have thought of asking her for it. In any case, she would have refused. "We're not cannibals!" she would have protested. Did she say it out loud? John Paradis looks up from his plate.

"Are you still thinking of that?"

"Of what?"

He smiles.

"Admit that it disturbed you. You should never have given her Christopher Columbus," he says, turning to Béatrice. "Now she's traumatized by the idea that the Indigenous ate their fellow men."

Béatrice speaks of the protein content—very import- ant. She and John Paradis burst out laughing. What or who are they laughing about? Her mind elsewhere, Marjolaine has trouble concentrating. *It's her they're making fun of*, she thinks. She feels mortified. Especially after her conversation with John Paradis earlier. Yet he'd seemed to understand her, had even spoken of her charm. And the latest news was no joking matter. The young woman who died, far too young. It's as if he has forgotten her. Marjolaine is not really in the mood for celebrating.

"You're laughing at me," she says.

"With you," Béatrice says.

Except that Marjolaine isn't laughing.

"I read in a book that hell would be paradise for foodies," Béatrice says. "They'll spend eternity stoking the flames beneath enormous stockpots."

"Stockpots in which their fellow men are simmering—gourmets or gourmands like themselves."

"Or else ascetics, as thin as rakes. And paradise is a kind of hell where people will no longer have any desire, any hunger."

"But hunger is monstrous!" John Paradis says.

"Not when it's sated. It's thanks to hunger that we have so much pleasure eating."

"What's the title of your book? I definitely want to read it."

Béatrice thinks. "A medieval detective novel," she says. "No, from the Renaissance." She's forgotten the title. But she'll find it.

Always talking about books, those two. A professor of literature and a librarian, not surprising. Nevertheless, Marjolaine sometimes feels excluded from the conversation. Overlooked. Abandoned. Three is a bad number: she has always known. Without them, however, she'd be eating alone at her table, or with strangers who'd speak other languages and it would be even more unpleasant. John Paradis is nicer when Béatrice isn't there. And

Béatrice speaks to her of things she understands. Because she is not an imbecile. It's just that she hasn't had the time to read as many books as them.

Other diners now enter the room: the young married couple, some Asians, the British novelist and her three companions. A group of Muslims—the women are wearing hijabs—with their children.

Then the chess players sit down at the table next to them. Marjolaine wonders who won today. John Paradis is inclined to favour the bearded one.

"Barbarossa," Béatrice says, guffawing.

"No, Barbarussia."

"Russia?" Marjolaine is surprised. "Why?"

"They speak Russian together. I recognized the sounds. Russian, Polish, Bulgarian, in any case, a Slavic language."

"Cyrillic," Béatrice says.

Cyrillic, now. Whatever.

"Cyrillic is the alphabet, Béatrice. Not the language."

"Of course. I was joking."

Béatrice now checks the dessert menu.

"Oh! Opera cake!" she says.

John orders a cognac with his coffee. Marjolaine merely has a cup of tea.

* * *

The chess game is over. Stefan lost. Like most of the time, in fact. In his youth, he was rather talented. He belonged to a club in university, often won. He's rusty now. In Nessebar, there was no one to play with. Except for the computer, of course, but that can't be considered a person. And the computer is, to some extent, predictable. Not Lev Bromski. Lev Bromski is a formidable opponent, if not pitiless.

Stefan was private secretary to Ernesto Liri, a musician known for composing the music for a cult film, *Broken Wings*. Companion, confidant, private chauffeur for about fifteen years, in Nessebar, on the Black Sea, in Bulgaria. The old man—he was almost one hundred—is now deceased. He went over to the other side, with practically the grace of a Jean Cocteau character. Stefan saw neither a grimace nor an unsightly spasm on his face. He went peacefully: so much the better. A relief for him and for his family, in the end. It happened in Marina di Pisa, in Italy, last June. He wanted to revisit his part of the country before he died. He sensed death coming, that was obvious. Despite the end, it was a fine trip: there are no regrets. Liri was in heaven: he made a friend there, Costanza. She cooked him Tuscan dishes that reminded him of his childhood, *ribollita* and other peasant dishes that poor people eat. Like many Italians, he had known poverty in times past, and, curiously, it was as if he missed that misery now that he was rich. He who usually croaked had begun to coo like an adoring turtledove.

He had always been a gourmand and claimed that gluttony was not a sin. "More of an homage," he liked to say, "an homage to God and the kindnesses he continues to shower us with." He was a deep believer.

After Liri's death, Stefan put the last touches on the biography. He worked relentlessly, practically day and night. In two weeks, it was completed—he had devoted

himself to it for years unbeknownst to the party concerned, had only the last moments to add. He put the
finishing touches on the manuscript, reviewed it, and sent
it by registered mail to various publishers with a carefully written cover letter. Then he awaited the responses.

One publisher expressed interest: that was already
something. Stefan had contacted a good dozen of them.
Most didn't answer—but perhaps he was in too much of
a hurry. They hadn't even read it, he would swear to it.
You had only to see the form letter of the few who had
the grace to send him one. "We are sorry to ..." "Despite
definite qualities ..." "Unfortunately does not correspond
to our editorial policies." What contempt. And those who
read it—except for one—were not impressed. He imagines the reactions. Ernesto Liri? Some didn't even know
who he was. And those who knew found little interest in
publishing his story. A film score composer. Not really
exciting. He died at almost one hundred, okay, we have
him to thank for *Broken Wings*, okay too. He had lived
in Hollywood, alongside the greats and others who had
since fallen into oblivion, spent his final years in Bulgaria, which unquestionably had its importance, as the
book was written in Bulgarian. And so? Readers, not to
mention critics, were not going to rush to read it. The
book would remain on bookstore shelves, at least those
that agreed to take it, and in a year, perhaps two, the
unsold copies, that is almost the entire print run, were
fated to be pulped, the shameful end of most books.
Review copies would be sold at a discount in secondhand
bookstores. Time and money wasted, not to mention the
paper, even recycled. In a time of crisis, one could not
allow this kind of shameless waste.

Interest, however, was shown by a small publisher: Lev Pavlovitch Bromski in Rome, a Russian, but born and raised in Bulgaria. The publishing house was called Poluostrov, peninsula in Bulgarian, a reminder of the Balkans. It was not Stefan's first choice, but did he have any other? To begin with, Poluostrov published online and Stefan was old school: he wanted to see his work in actual paper, touch it. To his mind, virtual was ephemeral: he wanted to last.

After having conscientiously—it was to be hoped—read the manuscript, Bromski summoned him to his Sofia office to share his comments with him. His verdict: "Good, but too dry. Academic. You have to romanticize it. Add dialogue, invent it even. Put some life into it. Flesh on the carcass. Readers want flesh and blood. Sperm too, why not? And tears, of course. A lot of tears. He wants to have the impression of being there. Of identifying. Identifying is the keyword. For readers often lead dull lives, don't forget. Repeat the same old routine. Alas, that is the lot of most people. Books allow them to vicariously experience strong feelings of which they are deprived."

Stefan endured this. He had, however, arguments, other cards up his sleeve. He pointed out the importance of music in a film. In his opinion, it plays as vital a role as the screenplay, the actors, the director.

"Take *The Godfather*, take Sergio Leone's spaghetti westerns. It's the tune of *Man With a Harmonica* that gives all its power to *Once Upon a Time in the West*."

The other agreed.

"Of course, Stefan, I realize that. That's exactly why I want to publish this biography."

"It's in large part thanks to the music, to the theme song, that *Broken Wings* is an unforgettable film."

"You don't have to convince me. I'm already convinced. I'm a fan. Especially since the villain of the story is called Bromsky. With a *y*: English speakers always transform our Cyrillic *i* into a *y*. God knows why. But, no matter, it has always amused me."

"You identify with him?"

"Of course not ... Tell me the truth: am I as ugly as he?"

Stefan merely shook his head diplomatically. One thing is sure: *y* or *i*, neither of them were Adonises.

"So underhanded, so perverse," Bromski said. "I love this type of character more Machiavellian than life. When he terrorizes Lola, when he shoots down Stephen in the middle of the street, do you remember? Because the good guy in the story is called Stephen. What a coincidence, don't you think, Stefan, to find ourselves face to face, good and evil together? A sign of destiny."

Stefan admits that the coincidence has not escaped him either.

"Did it make you hesitate? Bromsky in the film is a kind of crook, the wolf who devours the two lambs."

"I don't think I'm a lamb."

"But perhaps I'm a wolf."

Stefan smiled.

"I'm ready to take the risk. And I know how to defend myself. You don't know what an animal I am. I, too, have claws and fangs."

"In any case, it's the coincidence that induced me to read you till the end."

The game was almost won.

He only had to convince him to publish his work in

book form. With, on the cover page, a photo of a younger Ernesto Liri, or, even better, with Lola—portrayed by Marjorie Martinez, his unforgettable muse. He imagined them, he at his piano, she in her black skirt and white blouse in front of a mirror, lipstick in hand, like in the movie's final scene.

"Where is our Lola?" Bromski suddenly asked.

"Right now, probably in Canada."

Bromski raised an eyebrow—he has very heavy ones, thick, red like his beard, bushy too—and Stefan explained to him that a young Canadian director had filmed or was filming, he wasn't quite sure what stage they were at, a remake of Robert Elkis' swan song. The film is to have a French title: *Lola la nuit*. According to what he understands, the director changed the story quite a bit. Vancouver will replace Southampton and the plot will now focus on the heroin trade and other misdeeds of the same ilk. In keeping with current tastes. We have to adapt to our times. Much more violent than the original, with more explicit scenes. Music by Nechaev, a Vancouver band. But Bromsky is still just as evil.

"Good. Nechaev, or Netchaïev, an old anarchist, I like that. He inspired the Narodnaya Volia movement, the People's Will ... My mother's name was Perovskaïa, you know."

Stefan reflected for a moment. Perovskaïa ... the name was familiar.

"Sofia Perovskaïa, a hard-line anarchist," Bromski said. "A very radical young woman. I am speaking of my mother's great grandmother's young cousin twice removed. She probably knew him. Netchaïev, I mean. She must have read his *Revolutionary Catechism*. She was twenty-seven when they hanged her with her accomplices for the assassination of Czar Alexander II ... She died young. Cover her face."

Seeing Stefan's disconcerted expression, he said: "*The Duchess of Malfi*, an English Renaissance play. I deserve no credit for knowing it: I'm a big fan of detective novels, particularly those of Mrs. Christie. She quotes that line in her *Sleeping Murder,* solved by the delightful Miss Marple. I never forgot it; I even had to read the original work. Agatha Christie, every publisher's dream." He sighed. "You know that, along with the Bible, she's still one of the best sellers of the world? ... According to witnesses, Sofia died heroically. Her head held high, if you can read that without irony in the case of death by hanging. But you were speaking of a remake."

"Lola will be played by a French-speaking Canadian, Marjorie Dubois, a rising star, and, going by the photos, very pretty. Even more so than the original, the first Marjorie. More delicate, less fleshy."

Bromski adopted a dreamy expression. Fleshy ... He, personally, likes it when women are curvaceous. He feels sorry for anorexics. Rather plump when she began, Marjorie Martinez ended up becoming that, if he goes by her last photos. In the end, the poor girl was lanky—skin and bones. What a waste. Drugs, despair. They had a fling, apparently, experienced passion. She and the director.

Just gossip, Stefan protested. Liri already confided to him that Robert Elkis liked them younger. Much younger.

"Well, well! He liked nymphets! A pedophile. Vladimir Nabokov so well described that ..."

"Pathology?"

"... in *Lolita*, one of my favourite books in my youth. I see. He wasn't the only one. They made less of a fuss about it at that time, whereas today. Can you imagine the scandal if a contemporary author took it into his head to write *Lolita*? Nabokov made his pedophile likeable: that's the entire strength of the novel. You will admit that Humbert is rather pitiful with his impossible love."

Stefan admitted it.

"This is the type of thing you should be talking about it in your book."

Bromski thought for a moment.

"I'm a fan," he said. "Both of the film and its music."

Another moment of silence. Then: "In spite of everything ... Ernesto Liri. It's not like it's about Napoleon, or Peter the Great, what have you. Or even about Lenin, Christopher Columbus, Che Guevara—people who influenced the history of the world. And in the end, even for them, do we really know? Their true motives, their emotions—they had them, surely, even the tyrants. Historians are obliged to imagine. They weren't there. So they embellish based on diaries, the memoirs of contemporaries, correspondence. Did Liri write?"

Stefan replied that to his knowledge, no, Liri did not write. He would have known; he was his secretary. To begin with, the poor man suffered from arthritis. His deformed hands could barely hold a pen. He never dictated anything to him aside from a few letters. He had never learned to use a computer. Said that, for him, there was only one keyboard and it was on a piano.

"No, he didn't write. But he spoke. Over the years, he confided many memories to me, genuine or invented. No way of knowing if what he told me was true. Memory is often unfaithful. In any case, I transcribed all that later, faithfully."

"Faithfully: perhaps that's the problem, Stefan. Who wants fidelity? To whom, to what do you want to be faithful?"

"To the truth."

"Who wants truth? Most of the time it's no match for our lies."

At the end of the meeting, Bromski suddenly asked if he played chess.

"Without being a champion, I can defend myself," Stefan said, modestly.

"Wonderful. I'm leaving on a cruise: ten days in the Cyclades. My brother was supposed to come with me, but he's broken his leg. An unfortunate fall on his staircase. The ship lifts anchor in three days from Venice. Are you free?"

"As a bird."

≈ Their conversation gave Stefan an idea. Ernesto Liri had left him the house in Nessebar as well as a substantial amount of money. He'd always been generous. Nevertheless, the others, the family, wore gloomy expressions when the will was read. Liri had rewritten his will in Tuscany. His granddaughter Vittoria, Vickie, present right here, on the ship, with her henchman, a tattooed and rather hefty Argentine, inherited the rights to *Broken Wings,* the cash cow. And for a long time to come, if the tendency continues. Not hard to guess how she'll blow her inheritance, because blow it she will. It will all be spent on white powder and other forbidden pleasures. What's more, pregnant out to here. Stefan can scarcely imagine the baby's fate. But Vittoria, it's strange. She was not the patriarch's favourite: far from it. Who knows, perhaps he felt guilt at having loved her so little during his lifetime. He left money to Maria and her family who took care of the house—and of him—in Nessebar. Ten thousand euros to Constanza, "her *ribollita* was divine," seven hundred thousand to "Stefan, my loyal friend for all these years," in addition to the Bulgarian house. The rest of his fortune was divided equally among his children. He forgot no one.

But after this bequest, there wasn't much left, it must be admitted. Crumbs—rights to films no longer shown in cinematheques or even on TV late at night. Flops: let's not mince words. One of his daughters wanted to contest the will. "He was no longer rational, that's obvious." But he was indeed rational, and Vittoria's father was opposed. Some took one side, some the other. A free-for-all in the notary's office, with shouting, tears, and gnashing of teeth. But Stefan doesn't mention that in the book. Because: "Above all, don't involve living people," Bromski insisted. "Only the dead. We don't want to be sued for libel."

On the ship, Vickie, strangely, ignores him, acts like she doesn't recognize him. When he greeted her, the first day, she turned her head away. Since then, he's acted as if he doesn't recognize her either. She must be angry at him, she too, for the seven hundred thousand euros that were nevertheless well deserved. Or she coveted the beautiful house in Nessebar, feels wronged. Or it's something else. She has always been disturbed. All flocks have their black sheep: among the Liris its name is Vittoria.

When he receives his bequest, in about ten months,

perhaps a year or even more—these formalities require time—Stefan could of course self-publish. He doesn't want to; it's recognition he desires. To be in the limelight after all the years spent in the shadows. He has other plans.

He reviewed the manuscript the first five nights of the cruise. He began by jazzing up Liri's story, putting some flesh on the carcass, as Bromski demanded. Easier said than done. A torrid affair with an icon, perhaps? There he didn't lack for choice. Ava? Marilyn? Greta? No, Greta Garbo was stretching things: no one would believe him. As cold as ice, according to what people say. Besides, she'd already left Hollywood in the fifties. As for Ava, she wrote her autobiography without ever mentioning his name. He hesitated, then chose Marilyn. The idea had actually come to him at Ernesto Liri's bedside as he lay dying. It was plausible, everything was, and it didn't hurt anyone as both parties were dead and buried. Perhaps it had even happened, who knows? The old man had never spoken of it, but did he tell everything? Everyone is entitled to his mysteries, large or small. Perhaps he'd forgotten large parts of his life—although an affair with Marilyn would likely be etched in his memory in indelible ink.

On the morning of the sixth day, before their first game of chess, he handed his new version to the publisher. The verdict would come today.

"This time, you could have won," Bromski said.

After looking at the menu, he closed it and placed it on the table. Their choice was made. Standing by, the maître d' awaits their order.

To begin, they will share the assortment of mezze—

Bromski calls them zakuskis—hummus, tzatziki, htipipi, baba ghanouj, black Kalamata olives. Bromski asks whether they have Baltic Sea sprats. With black bread, they're delicious. They do not, nor have they any black bread, but there are sardines in olive oil, marinated herring, and smoked sturgeon. And white bread. He chooses the sturgeon. Then, for him, a grilled pepper steak, rare, and moussaka for Stefan. All of this washed down with a bottle of iced vodka.

"When you moved your bishop ... it would have been better to sacrifice your rook."

Stefan visualizes their game. Yes, that move was a mistake: he'd realized it almost right away. He'd moved with too much haste; he'd been excited this morning. Two moves later, the black knight took his queen. And without the queen, the king, that oaf, is cornered, unable to defend himself. An ordinary pawn defeated him.

A girl in a black skirt and white blouse approaches with a carafe and pours water into their glasses. Then two waiters arrive, one with the vodka which he serves and then places in a bucket of ice while the other sets down a basket of bread beside them. The plate of mezze is placed in the middle of the table. Bromski raises his glass.

"To Ernesto Liri!"

And swallows it in one go. He waves the waiter away, signifying to him that they'll serve themselves.

"Let's move on to serious things, my dear Stefan. The biography ... I reread it carefully and believe I like the changes you've made. However, you'll say I'm repeating myself, but I still find the main character too dull. For the book to enjoy the success it deserves, you have to make our musician more mysterious, sexier. Even dangerous."

Stefan mentally shrugs his shoulders. Liri was harmless. Only someone who never knew him could imagine him presenting the slightest danger.

"He was Italian. Perhaps he had ties to the Mafia," Bromski says. "Like Frank Sinatra, for instance."

"He never spoke to me of any. Nor of Sinatra, in fact."

He was indeed in the US during the witch-hunt. Bromski wants to know if, perchance, he had sympathies with the Communist party. But Stefan ensures him that politics did not interest him. He was completely allergic.

"Too bad. It would make him interesting."

The mezze dispatched with, the steak and the moussaka are placed before the guests. Bromski asks for another basket of bread.

"We'll surely find something, don't you worry. By the way, I very much liked the slightly racy passage with Marilyn."

"Completely invented. At least, I think so. Perhaps he didn't tell me everything about his private life."

"Invent other episodes. Titillating, racy, even scandalous affairs, so readers have something to sink their teeth into. Make them dream. What if you involved the Kennedy brothers, for example? Women find those tall blonds romantic; men want to be like them. Without the assassinations, of course. Although I'm not so sure. Admit that the thing has a certain ... how to say? A certain panache ... A heroic death. And filmed live. People are still talking about it more than fifty years later."

Stefan nods his head, doubtful. The Kennedy brothers? It could be pushing things—even though the idea had occurred to him in Italy while Ernesto Liri lay dying. He'd rejected it quickly. In that case, why not an affair with Jackie Bouvier? Or even Maria Callas, once he's making things up. Liri composed a song for the diva—that she of course refused. Bromski pours them some vodka, raises his glass again.

"Now, let's move onto more serious things: your project."

The project, there it is, as Stefan presented it to Lev Bromski, giving him the reworked manuscript: when he receives the money bequeathed by Ernesto Liri, he'd like to invest it, partially, at least, in Poluostrov's publishing house. He'd like to create, direct a new collection—in book form, of course—of fictional biographies. He already has some ideas. He wants characters who have influenced history and that history, ungrateful and inaccurate as it too often is, seems to have excluded from its memory. Characters that it scorns or avoids. Not important enough. Insignificant. And inventing others who never existed—or perhaps they did—give them a role to play.

"But that's already been done and redone," Bromski now says. "Take Dumas and his musketeers, Captain Altavista by Perez-Reverte. And even that English novelist, you know, Hope Spencer. She's here, on our ship, sailing with us."

He bursts out laughing. Stefan smiles slightly. The publisher must be talking about that heavyset woman, getting on in years, who wears a different hat every day. What's more, the day before yesterday, the wind carried away her lilac boater. It resembled an Easter egg at sea. Was it her?

Bromski dunks a piece of bread in the pepper sauce. His mouth full, he indicates yes.

"Even she had a go at it. The loves of Archduke

Rudolf and Mary Vetsera inspired her to turn out one of her first little works, never republished, at least I hope not. The affair or the mystery of Mayerling became, under her pen, dipped in schmaltz, naturally: *Viennese Waltz in F Minor.* I read it long ago. I read a lot and not only good books, alas. I have to know what the public likes and doesn't like; my job as a publisher requires these sacrifices."

Stefan assents silently.

"And she's not the only one," Bromski says. "I could cite dozens of authors who were inspired by the affair. Middle-aged women are crazy about these stories of persecuted sweethearts, of damned lovers. It used to be young girls looking for Prince Charming who lapped up sentimental novels. They've smartened up; now their cocktails are stronger. They want nuance. Pale or dark grey."

Stefan remains silent.

"Look," Bromski says. "I recently read a fairly twisted novel in which Sigmund Freud is the hero. He and Jung are invited to New York in 1909 to deliver lectures. During their stay, sordid murders are committed. Men in tailcoats bind girls hand and foot, whip them then strangle them with their tie. Did it really happen? I admit I checked on the Internet. The lectures on psychoanalysis indeed were given that year. But the murders were never mentioned on the sites I consulted. Did they take place? You'll answer me that crimes of this kind have been committed in all times, that dozens of girls are strangled every year in all cities over the world. So why not in New York in 1909? Why not, in fact? The author simply associated a historical event, the lectures, with real or invented murders. And I'm not even speaking of the interminable dialogues on the Oedipus complex between Carl Jung and Freud in a hotel room. We have to take the novelist at his word: he wasn't present. And I'll tell you that deep down I couldn't care less because while I'm reading, I believe it, and that's all that matters to me. And I think of that other one in which Queen Blanche of Castile—"

"You're talking about novels, Lev Pavlovitch," Stefan says, interrupting. "My collection will only publish biographies. Why do people always remember the names of tyrants, dictators, conquerors—Nero, Hitler, Stalin, Hernán Cortés? Personally, I'd prefer a biography of his Aztec interpreter, Malinche, of whom we know virtually nothing. Who speaks of her? Who knows her? Yet she was the *lengua*, the language of the conquistador. He mentions her in his letters to the Catholic Kings. He even had a son with her, Martín, whom he recognized, the first mestizo officially recorded—who probably ended his days in a Spanish dungeon. Without Malinche, Cortés would have been defeated, I assure you. He didn't stand a chance. She was the heart of the affair. Without her, no conquest of Mexico."

Bromski nods his head, chews his meat, wipes his lips with his napkin.

"The story of the model rather than the one of the painter," Stefan says, fervently. "I'm thinking of that gentleman from Seville."

"What gentleman?"

"We don't know, actually. There's a painting people believe was done by Murillo, in the Louvre, currently.

Was the gentleman in question even from Seville? Some claim he lived in Madrid and that Murillo never went there. How to know after all these years? How to verify?"

"And how do you come to know all that?"

"Apparently, a woman in France had the painting, true or false," Stefan says, having seen a report on that extortion. "They starved her, tortured her, for stealing it from him. Or think of Mona Lisa. Who knows who she really was, what she felt while she was posing for the painting? In the end all we know is her enigmatic smile."

"The smile that enchants us."

And Bromski gives an outline of a smile that has nothing enchanting about it, given his awful teeth.

"The disciple, the servant rather than the master," Stefan says, "the victim rather than his assassin. You know the name of Landru."

"Who doesn't?"

"But do you know the names of the women he reduced to ashes in his stove? Even one? Do you even know how many he knocked off?"

"About ten?"

Another approximation. Stefan suppresses a gesture of impatience.

Perhaps the assassins are more interesting than the victims, suggests Bromski, the monsters more than their servants. Unless the servants in turn become masters or assassins. More interesting from a novelistic point of view, it goes without saying. But Stefan sticks firmly to his position: he prefers the obscure third violin in a provincial orchestra humbly playing his score in a Beethoven symphony to Beethoven himself about whom everything has already been said.

"Has everything really been said? Besides, it's Beethoven who fascinates people."

"An anonymous grenadier during the Russian campaign, an unknown soubrette screwed on the sly rather than the great Napoleon."

"Great ... According to what we know about him, the mythomaniac was small of stature ... But ... soubrette, grenadier ..."

Lev Pavlovitch caresses his red beard. Frankly, no, he doesn't really see the interest.

"No, not written like novels," Stefan says, "but like very serious works, documented, scientific, with a preface, footnotes, and an exhaustive bibliography at the end. A kind of allusion to history."

"Yes, and I'm seeking readers."

"We'll find them, Lev Pavlovitch."

"My friends call me Liova."

His friends? So there's hope?

"We were speaking of Napoleon. If you read the account of the war he led in Spain, you'll learn that a young officer was nailed, upside down, to a barn door," Stefan says. "A little farther on, three exhausted soldiers committed suicide, terrorized by the idea of being captured by the Spanish."

"They'd probably learned the fate reserved for your young officer. But you have only to go to the Prado and see *The Disasters of War* by that admirable painter — Goya, to understand that when it comes to cruelty, the French had nothing on the Spanish. War, alas, awakens the basest instincts of the human race."

"A young officer, unhappy peasants, three soldiers. They didn't even have names. History swallowed them up."

"Cannon fodder," Lev Bromski says.

Cannon fodder: Stefan detests that expression. Anonymous flesh. But that young officer had a family, perhaps a fiancée waiting for him in France. Were they even told of the horrible way he died? What do people know of him? And then only if they read the same book as he —just one sentence sufficed to describe his martyrdom. Whereas we know about the tyrant's slightest heartburn.

Suddenly Stefan seems discouraged. He rubs his right eye. But the image of the crucified young man two centuries ago resists, as if imprinted on his retina. I'll give you a name, he swears, teeth clenched. I'll give you a life. I'll describe your slow death; I'll describe your cruel death. You won't have suffered in vain. Bromski fills their glasses. Around them, waiters circulate with plates. A woman bursts out laughing. A baby cries.

"The footnotes of history are the only history that's real ... Liova, written by little people. With their blood, as you say, their sperm, their tears."

"You're sensitive, Stefan ... That's not a criticism."

But Stefan has recovered.

"We could even write about your relative. Sofia Perovskaïa. People know so little about her."

Bromski stops him: it's already been done. A certain Leo Arnchtam even made a film about her.

"Reinvent her life," Stefan says. "Give her a passionate love for, I don't know, Bakunin, Netchaïev."

"She had a lover. They were hanged together."

"So write about that love."

But Bromski says no; he'd prefer to leave the family out of that. They wouldn't understand, could feel hurt or even betrayed.

"Times are hard for us publishers, you know. Nowadays people prefer video games, ephemeral things like that. And those who read only want stories of serial killers. You propose to publish the biography of illustrious unknowns. Novelists have been doing that since novels began. Or to invent those of illustrious people. Then it's biographers who have a great time. Whatever they say, biographies are always subjective, that is to say fictional. I repeat: I'm seeking readers."

Stefan has no answer to give. Then: "Just so, Liova. The reader will believe my fictional biographies."

"We still have to find authors to write them."

"I'll find them. Otherwise, I'll write them myself. All of them. One a year. I'll use pseudonyms."

Bromski sighs. People want to read great stories. Blood, sperm, and tears were the bread and circuses of the ancient Romans.

"Don't believe that humanity has changed," he says.

"I know well that it hasn't changed. But the footnotes of history are the only history that's real," Stefan says again. "The only one written with blood and tears. The other is just a collection of dates of battles lost or won. A chronicle devoid of soul."

"And you, do you have a soul?"

Stefan hesitates for a microsecond, then: "Yes."

"So there are at least two of us ... But why does history need a soul?"

Stefan thought for a moment. "To become civilized, perhaps. We remember the tyrants, and when it comes to the victims, we give approximate figures, five million dead, a hundred thousand, ten thousand, three hundred, depending on the battle or the attack."

"We know of one victim: the unknown soldier," Bromski says with a little smile.

But Stefan does not smile.

"I was speaking seriously. The unknown soldier, indeed, why not? I want to give the victims a voice. To do them this justice. I want to give the anonymous ones a name. They say history repeats itself, but I believe it's historians who repeat themselves. When they're ordered to write something, they all end up writing the same thing."

A waiter removes their plates. Another hands them the dessert menu. They don't want any; they've eaten enough, don't have a sweet tooth. They ask for two strong espressos, an apricot rakija for Stefan, a plum one for Bromski.

It's always the victors who write history, continues Stefan. The defeated are dead, and the survivors would rather forget it. It always depends on the storyteller. Everything's a matter of interpretation. And he wants to interpret it in his way.

Bromski believes it is also written by the defeated, through the resentment of the defeated that has ruminated sometimes for centuries, in secret. The survivors never forget ... He falls silent for a moment, then has an idea. Why not a collection of historical detective novels, he suggests, reassured. At present, the genre is working very well.

Stefan shakes his head. His collection will publish biographies: he stands by that. Even though, of course, there will be crime and punishment in them.

Their coffees and liqueurs drunk, they stand up and go walk on the deck. Bromski lights a cigar, like the

Bromsky of the film in an unforgettable scene. Stefan no longer smokes.

"Admit that it's contradictory," Bromski says. "You want to publish fictional biographies, and for Liri, you hesitate to depart from the historical truth, if I can put it that way."

"Ernesto Liri isn't a fictional character. He truly existed; I lived by his side. I don't wish to betray him. At least, not betray him too much. This biography will be the only authentic one. But it will not be in my collection."

"Don't say that."

Bromski stops, contemplates for a moment, then: "You know, you almost had me convinced, Stefan. Almost."

Stefan holds his breath.

"Begin by revising Liri's biography. Give him wings. From wherever he is, in heaven or in hell ..."

Stefan would rather see him in heaven. Even if he does not believe in one or the other.

"You know what, Stefan? I think people who say they are atheists do so because they're afraid of having to spend eternity singing hymns."

"Or burning. In the end, I still prefer Earth, despite all its faults."

"In any case, wherever he is, Liri won't criticize you. He may even be flattered for becoming the character that you invent."

Both are leaning on ship's rail, gazing at the blue sea.

"In the end, you're a utopian, Stefan. You dream in colour."

"An idealist," Stefan says, correcting him. "And a dreamer, true."

"Yes, an idealist; I envy you that. Personally, I'm a realist. Just a modest bookseller."

Modest bookseller! Now he is laying it on. Bromski isn't modest; far from it.

"But dreamers need realistic men," he says. "And vice-versa ... We need one another."

They take a few steps toward the table where they played this morning. The chessboard is still there.

"Well Stefan, do you want that rematch?"

6

The Beyond, at Some Point in Eternity

There is no justice ...

She must have read his Revolutionary Catechism.

*According to what he understands, the director
changed the story quite a bit.*

THE BEYOND IS in turmoil.

At the bottom of oblivion, Francis Lafargue, unjustly ignored author of detective stories, stamps his feet and fumes. Not only had that two-faced Bob Elkis massacred his work in times past, but now a pretentious young fellow, a total unknown, has gotten into his head to film a remake of *Broken Wings* in the depths of Canada. And he has done so: the film will be screened in various festivals all year long. *Lola la nuit.* A pedantic, pompously intellectual title. Lafargue detests that. He hadn't dared protest when Bob Elkis titled the film *Broken Wings*. He'd chafed. Because, at the time, he was full of hope, saw himself walking the shining path of glory. He thought he was making a great deal, the deal of his life. Think of it: a star director, the darling of Hollywood had bought —for practically nothing—the rights to his detective novel, and the film would be shot in America, no less. Well, he came down to earth very quickly. The monster mutilated his work, massacred everything. And *Broken Wings* was an allusion to the broken wings of the insignificant Lola, the lead, whereas in his book she was only a secondary character. Less than secondary. An extra. The odious Bromsky was in the forefront, and with him, Frank Dilo, the recurring private detective—he showed up in about fifteen of his novels. Frank Dilo, Frankie to his friends, a great lover of tequila and chain smoker of Gitanes, as it should be. Elkis had eliminated him from the screenplay.

Broken Wings and now *Lola la nuit*—Lola again. He, Francis Lafargue, a simple man, had simply titled it *Imbroglio in Southampton*. Or was it trouble? No, trouble was in Bruges. Or in Lisbon? Imbroglio or trouble, in the end, it's the same. An unpretentious title; he never took himself for someone he was not. It's now set in Vancouver. In his book the imbroglio or trouble took place in Southampton. And Bromsky has become a heroin trafficker. What rubbish. Elkis at least kept the theft of the van even if he retained nothing else. But was it in that novel, the theft of the van? He feels as if he's been losing his memory for some time. It's natural to forget when you're in oblivion.

Like the last time, his name does not even appear in the credits. Whereas he is nevertheless the source of all this excitement. When the film came out, Elkis at most had admitted in a few interviews that he had been "freely" inspired by a mediocre detective novel. A "pallid detective novel" or "pâle polar" as he had described it—in French. And everyone had found that hilarious, even those who didn't speak the language repeated it. An irresistible play on words. Blasted Bob, what a sense of humour. A born joker. That guy is priceless. Laughing at others, yes, he never denied himself that. And everyone went into ecstasies in the face of his genius. Now, the interloper struts around nirvana while he himself vegetates, rotting in oblivion since God knows how long—well God, in a manner of speaking, where he is, no one has ever seen his shadow, if he has one. Perched at the top of his kingdom, the Eternal does certainly not sink to frequent the plebs in the lower depths. No, here time does not exist. Everything stretches out, everything is grey, you die of boredom. If only you could die. But you're already dead. Lafargue tells himself sometimes that existence is perhaps more pleasant in hell, if indeed it exists. Even though it appears that people there suffer a lot. Dante invented all kinds of tortures for the damned. And, although he himself enjoyed inventing them in his books, he shivers when he thinks he hears the exiles screaming in their cauldron.

In his naïveté he thought ... hoped ... that this time they'd do him justice. But no. A vain hope. The young fellow, Nicholas something, took up Bob Elkis' work: that's what the newspapers say. As if *Broken Wings* could have existed without him, Francis Lafargue. There is no more justice in the beyond than there was here below. That is, over there. Because here below is now here, at the bottom of oblivion, and you can't go down any farther. No, justice does not exist. Nor does it in his novels and half the time it was the treacherous who won. Unless Frank Dilo set things right. But an innocent, most often a woman, always died before he entered the scene. That's how it is in life as well.

He's bitter, it's true, but who wouldn't be in his

position? He did his work honestly when he was on earth, without showing off or bowing and scraping. He didn't claim to be a genius, didn't take himself for Shakespeare or Dante, had but one goal: to entertain people. Honesty does not pay, and he proved that as well more than once in his books where the lambs succumbed more often than the wolves. Let's be clear: fiction never surpasses reality.

Yet he is not asking for the moon. Just that Caesar be given his due. At the very least the minimal recognition he deserves. But even this is denied him. In the Olympus of detective novelists, it's as if there's only room left for the ubiquitous Agatha Christie accompanied by her creatures: Marple and her knitting, Poirot and his grey cells, mustache, and patent leather shoes—unlikely detectives, if you ask his opinion.

He had, however, felt some hope the other day. On a cruise ship, a bookseller found a copy, rather worn, it's true, of his thriller and read it. A bookseller. All was not lost, then. Who knows? She could recommend it to her clients, order it, if any copies remained, for her bookstore, even second-hand. A new publisher could be interested in it, a new edition would be published, with that title— *Bluffing* or *Trouble*—and others, in a boxed set, perhaps. Such a thing has already happened and that's how artists unjustly banished managed to emerge from oblivion. Well, no. Like the others, the bookseller had only contemptuous comments about his work. A drugstore novel. And why not. He's not ashamed of it. You need them to pass the time in a train, especially as in his day, high-speed trains did not exist. Insignificant writing, she decreed starkly before placing *Imbroglio in Southampton*—was it indeed *Imbroglio*?—on its shelf. Perhaps he should rejoice: at least she didn't throw it into the Aegean.

He paces back and forth on the viscous ground of oblivion when suddenly ... Oh! No! Here's that blue-stocking, the devil take her, poetess, as she calls herself, Régine or Germaine something, he never remembers and couldn't care less—here she comes.

Even she is in dire straits.

"A remake of *Broken Wings*," she yells at the top of her voice, pacing up and down oblivion. "As if it were possible to remake a masterpiece."

A masterpiece.

Too late; she's noticed him. Nowhere to hide. She rushes toward him dramatically.

"Monsieur Lafigue!"

Always massacring his name, that one.

"Fargue!" he shouts.

"Monsieur Fargue, yes ..."

"Lafargue!"

"Please excuse me, Monsieur Fa ..."

"Lafargue!"

"Lafargue, yes. I have no memory for names. Especially because now I'm stunned, filled with dismay, appalled, di—"

"I understand," he says, interrupting.

Otherwise she'll go through the entire thesaurus. And he has even less patience than usual today.

"You've heard the news, Monsieur Laforgue?"

"Yes," he replies, as curtly as possible.

"They've dared touch *Broken Wings*."

"I know."

"They even replaced the music, the unforgettable song composed by Ernesto Liri. They dared."

Well, she hasn't forgotten that one's name. She's not very well going to begin singing. Well, yes. He blocks his ears.

"It's a … punk or whatever band now doing the music."

He must admit that Liri's little song wasn't bad. It's the only thing he'll admit. The music is now by a band called Nechaev. Nechaev or Netchaïev, Nechayev, regardless of how it's written—in any case a Russian name, is also in nirvana with his *Revolutionary Catechism*. An assassin who killed a man with his own hands, one Ivanov —who remembers him? The unfortunate must be hanging around oblivion while the others, thieves and assassins, hold forth and congratulate one another in nirvana. And meanwhile he, Francis Lafargue, a writer unjustly ignored, fulminates and ruminates in his hole.

≈ But in nirvana people do not only congratulate themselves. Things do not consistently go smoothly. Robert Elkis—he entered there without even going through purgatory despite all his sins—is also fuming. And Marjorie Martinez is sobbing.

"I was not anorexic."

"Of course not. You ate like a bird, that's all."

"Lola is me," she says, moaning, inconsolable.

"Of course it's you," Elkis says with a sigh, patting her shoulder.

"There's even someone, down there, who says that

the other one, the new one, is prettier than me. He calls me fleshy."

"Fleshy and anorexic, you can see they contradict one another. They're talking nonsense."

"Yes, but ..."

"You know the saying: sticks and stones may break my bones ..."

"Break my bones?"

"But words will never hurt me. Let them talk, my angel. You'll still always be the most beautiful."

That's what frightens her. She wonders: can people be demoted once they're in nirvana? She's heard of a place at the back of who knows where called oblivion, where a gang of forgotten languish. She's terrorized at the idea of one day finding herself relegated there. Because that's what could happen if the movie that made her immortal is ousted by the remake.

Bob Elkis is afraid of nothing; he is immortal and knows it. But he's furious at the slander people are beginning to spread about him. Pedophile! What will they come up with next? He was always faithful to his wife. Well, almost always. And his extremely rare affairs were not with nymphets. That all comes from that Stefan, the right-hand man, Ernesto Liri's flunkey, who swallowed the fairy tales the composer told him. But Liri had become senile, as was well known, at the end he'd lost his memory and said just about anything. His own fantasies, perhaps. Senile and jealous. Because he'd always been jealous. For while he had composed a nice tune—that, no one ever denied—it was not into his arms that women dreamed of falling. It was he, Robert Elkis, who had the charisma. In any case, it's cowardly to speak ill of people no longer around to defend themselves. All that's missing is an old frustrated starlet, ninety years old, to come out of the shadows to slander him. There were many of them flitting around him like fireflies, begging for a screen test. Many are called but few are chosen, alas. One of them could accuse him of indecent assault and other wrongdoings. Of misconduct, as they say nowadays. To get invited on talk shows, some people are prepared to do anything, especially the worst.

≈ As for Ernesto Liri, recently arrived in the beyond, he is oscillating between vexation and euphoria. That Stefan decided to tell about, even invent his life story does not displease him. That he had him have an affair with the divine Marilyn will not be cause for complaint, either. She's here, she as well, and is certainly in no danger of being demoted. The beauty does not have one wrinkle. He comes across her occasionally, always incredibly tantalizing in her polka dotted dress whose skirt flies up in the wind, revealing adorable little white panties. He'd also come across her on earth, in parties in Santa Monica, or Clara, he doesn't remember which, but she didn't recognize him. It must be said that at those parties the idol often had too much to drink. He's been led to understand that she's been portrayed as having sympathies to the communist party in the middle of McCarthyism, of rubbing shoulders with John Kennedy, another resident of nirvana. Glory, in fact. But that is not certain. The publisher suggested it: Stefan, too honest, is still hesitating. There is hope though: if it isn't one of the Kennedys, it will be someone else. Patience and time, as Shakespeare so aptly wrote. No, he is mixed up, Shakespeare didn't say that. It was Racine. Or Corneille. He'll find out. In any case, it was a Frenchman, in nirvana, and for a long time. He's anxious to see what Stefan will imagine. He trusts him, does not regret the seven hundred thousand euros he bequeathed him.

That's the positive side of things. What enrages him, however, is that the Vancouver filmmaker decided to change the music. As Stefan said so well: "It's in large part thanks to the music, to the theme song, that *Broken Wings* is an unforgettable film." And now scarcely a few notes, far too shrill, call to mind the original.

Everyone has done their version of the hymn, mariachis, opera tenors, a singer with green or blue hair, in all rhythms: tango, rock, jazz, flamenco. It's been translated into all languages, even Japanese. That's the price of glory; he accepted it, had nothing against it. Especially as it brought in more money than he needed. He even recognized his ditty, in Muzak version, in elevators and on the interminable telephone wait lines.

But to think they could remake the film, relinquishing his music, is simply inconceivable. It's no longer a remake; it's a massacre.

≈ Let's now see how the other protagonists described on the cruise ship are behaving. Morose, Hernán Cortés is smoking a cigar—still permitted in nirvana. A guy wants to make another movie about his story, *Noche triste*, and apparently, he won't be portrayed favourably. In the end, he couldn't care less. He was never really portrayed favourably, but he conquered Mexico, he's the father of it, and that no one is likely to forget. As for La Malinche, the conquistador's *lengua*, she is surely here, she too, hidden somewhere. And if she's not hidden, no one, except for Cortés, recognizes her.

Christopher Columbus merely smiles when he hears so-called experts speak of the Jewish origins of his father or mother, when he sees plaques placed in front of houses where he is supposed to have been born. Where was he born, in fact? Over time, perhaps he himself has forgotten.

As for Rudolf Hapsburg, he absolutely refuses to reveal the secret of his death. His mother Sissi goes around looking melancholy all the time.

One might believe Landru to be in hell. But people aren't sure there is one. Its existence has been called into question by some exegetes: it contradicts the very idea of a merciful God. Too bad for Dante and his torture. In any case, now people believe they can see the sinister figure of the killer of middle-aged women. Apparently, for the moment—if, however "moment" can apply to the concept of eternity—a space has been set up in nirvana for evil people like him, war criminals, sadists, and other torturers that history refuses to forget. Of course they do not enjoy the same privileges as the chosen; they don't wear the same white tunic or float upon the clouds, but they're there. As for the victims, they are, as could be expected, relegated to oblivion with the forgotten.

≈ While Ivanov, the presumed traitor, languishes at the bottom of oblivion, in fact, Sergueï Netchaïev seems very satisfied with his lot. But did he kill him with his hands? Apparently he commanded the execution, which is in the end the same thing. "I inspired Dostoevsky," he says, crowing. "I'm at the origin of *Demons*: Pyotr Verkhov-ensky is me!" The fact that a band of anarchist musicians took his name comforts him enormously. He paces back and forth brandishing his *Revolutionary Catechism*. "The nature of the true revolutionary excludes all senti-mentality, romanticism, infatuation, and exaltation," he recites. "All private hatred and revenge must also be excluded."

He's been repeating the same platitudes since he ar-rived, several years ago already. "He is not a revolution-ary if he has any sympathy for this world." The other chosen have grown tired of hearing him. He is alone today, fortunately. Because Bakunin sometimes joins him and when their two voices come together, a racket ensues.

"Will he shut up already?" Ernesto Liri says, exas-perated. "You can't hear yourself think around here any-more."

But Netchaïev isn't the type to shut up.

"The revolutionary is a doomed man. He despises public opinion. The nature of the true revolutionary ex-cludes all romanticism ..."

7

The *End of the World*, Early Afternoon

It was Béatrice who gave her Christopher Columbus.

On a cruise ship, a bookseller found a copy, rather worn, it's true, of his thriller and read it.

BÉATRICE TURNS ON her laptop. Not to work, no. She's on vacation. Nor to read the news: it's always bad. Out of habit, rather. To feel — or look — busy. In fact, she's here to think, to gather her thoughts as she does every afternoon. To place her thoughts in order — because for six months, it's been chaos in her head. These moments are sacred to her; she doesn't want to be disturbed. She doesn't need a pretext, but today she has one: she promised John Paradis she would find the title of that detective novel from the Middle Ages or the Renaissance that they talked about at lunch. In her computer, she has a file where she notes and comments on everything she reads; she doesn't want to forget anything. She must have read that one last summer. She remembers she brought it to Paradise Island with two or three others.

At this time of day, she is all alone in the ship's library. But there are never many people here: most are busy with other things. The slim Englishman consults his works here; the two Russians—or Poles, Bulgarians—sometimes play chess here in the morning or the evening, when the daily show is in full swing. That's about it. It's too hot on the deck at two in the afternoon. Too much sun. And, for a bookseller like herself, the library is a favourite spot. Surrounded by books, she feels at home. She works in a second-hand bookstore, Outre-mots, beyond words, in Outremont. An easy play on words, but she neither invented nor chose it.

She has an occupation that is in danger, she sometimes thinks. Dying out, like they say about species. People no longer read like they used to. Not so long ago, when she took the subway, she'd see one passenger out of two with their nose in a book. It was the same on café terraces: solitary clients read or pretended to read. To not look too lonely, no doubt. Now, they're all tapping away on their phones—they call them smartphones, and the notion that a telephone can be called smart is beyond her. The meaning of words keeps on changing. Gaiety no longer has anything to do with a good mood or cheerfulness. A cougar is no longer the proud feline that it was. In English, they even changed the name of that virile detective, Dante Sullivan—another Dante—in trendy police show that she's never watched. But she knows he was called the cougar and that he became a jaguar (in French he remained what he was). A cougar is now a middle-aged woman who seeks out gigolos—you wonder what the demoted wildcat thinks of its metamorphosis.

At least forests are now protected, she thinks, consoling herself. Trees can grow, wild animals take shelter. And wolves devour the does with impunity. A thought that is rather less comforting. But nature is what it is, and

Eden, the paradise that Christopher Columbus never stopped searching for, where lions and gazelles slept in each other's paws, is just another myth. For had Eden existed, surely it would not have taken in predators, wolves, tigers, and crocodiles. Otherwise what would they have eaten there—grass and fruit?

For the cruise, she brought a book, a biography of Christopher Columbus, precisely, which had spent months on the bookstore's shelves without ever finding a taker. She'd nevertheless displayed it in the window at the beginning, then placed in prominently on the mantelpiece—there is a purely decorative fireplace at Outre-mots—then on the coffee tables around which clients sit to leaf through a book before deciding if they're going to buy it or not. But it was a lost cause: no one wanted it. She had to resign herself to placing it in the clearance bin at two for a dollar—it breaks her heart each time—with no more success.

So, taking pity, she brought the explorer on the voyage, had him make the journey in reverse, from America to the Mediterranean of his birth.

A fictionalized biography, no doubt. Because, in the end, what do we really know about him other than he discovered America in 1492 when he thought he'd arrived in India? Not much. Almost nothing despite the hundreds of works devoted to him. What he wrote in his letters, what his biographer son wrote about him. But, in his letters, he said what he wanted. His son, too. Our history is filled with grey areas. Who killed the president? Who was hidden behind the iron mask? What happened to this one or that one who appeared for an instant to change the course of things, then disappeared, as if swallowed up, returned to nothingness?

America had been discovered long before he arrived, everyone knows that. The Natives who lived there for centuries, the Basques and Vikings who fished for cod off the Great Banks of Newfoundland. They just neglected to plant their flag on the shore.

She devoured it in two days, and then Marjolaine entered the library one morning, looking for something to read. Béatrice offered her Christopher Columbus. Marjolaine, the cook from the End of the World, Rue Saint-Zotique in Montreal, where she herself had her weekly meetings with Dante. She called him Dante in her head or Mister D—no, that was her friend Cora when she wanted to make fun of her. He never told her his name.

In this library, she hasn't found much to sink her teeth into. Books in all languages, perhaps, but in French ... two or three romance novels with yellowed pages, a tacky detective novel entitled *Imbroglio in Southampton* by one Lafargue. Insignificant writing, nothing very exciting. Francis Lafargue, an illustrious unknown who must be moping in oblivion with his fellow men, hacks, rhymesters, unskilled painters and forgotten singers. A drudge, that's the word. He wrote drugstore novels, as they used to say. A kind of candy to suck on during a trip. This imbroglio nevertheless reminded her of a black and white film that everyone had to see at least once, like *Casablanca*. The names of the characters most of all: Bromsky, Lola. An old film with a sad song that people still sing in all languages. The director perhaps took his inspiration from it, who knows? *Broken Wings*, that's it!

She did some research and, yes, Robert Elkis had indeed admitted he was inspired by a "pallid detective novel"—it must be that one. Pallid detective novel! She had a good laugh. So did John Paradis when she told him.

In English, she came across a copy of the bestseller *Fifty Shades of Grey*, but she finds reading in English difficult. Besides, she already read it in French in a so-so translation. She didn't mention it to anyone—she would have been a bit embarrassed. To tell the truth, those practices of submission, bondage and all that, are not really her thing. Reading it, nevertheless, did arouse strong feelings in her. Still gives her shivers when, at night, to fall asleep, she allows herself to imagine being tied up, gagged while a man, Dante or Max, or a regular of the bookstore, a passenger on the ship, whips and abuses her. She's gone through all the passengers in her head. The little Englishman, the one who sits with the novelist at teatime? No, not really. Imagination still has its limits. Him in leather, a riding crop in his hand? She'd burst out laughing and that's not the goal. The tattooed Argentine, on the other hand, makes her fantasize. Between the two chess players, she hesitates. Each has their charm. She finds something both primitive and good-natured about the bearded one; the other one is more mysterious. Why not both at once? Even John Paradis—JP. Although, with him, she favours situations that are more tender, classic, as it were, curled up against his shoulder, breathing in the aroma of his pipe—he lights one, at night, on the ship deck—of his vetiver cologne. They are merely dreams, daydreams, like when you count sheep—she tried, it never worked—dreams you conjure up when you can't sleep. In real life, she'd never agree to submit to torture.

She is not, will not be that type of woman: it's just a game. It's only to fall asleep that she imagines the torments—in times past people would go watch torture, see gladiators kill one another in the arena, heretics burned alive. The ogre and the wolf have always fascinated children. You love me when I suffer; I love you when you make me suffer. Or vice versa. Like Marguerite Duras. It's only when she can't sleep. Everyone is entitled to their secrets.

≈ So, Marjolaine, the cook from the greasy spoon. Kicked out in early summer without further ado. They recognized one another, without being entirely sure at the beginning. They knew they'd already seen one another, but where? Clients of one or the other. Did Marjolaine visit the bookstore? No. Did Béatrice frequent the *End of the World*? Well, yes. Not really frequented it, she'd go occasionally. Oh! That's where we saw one another. Marjolaine told her of her difficulties, voice quivering with annoyance, rage; Béatrice told her of her own, the fall on the sidewalk one evening last March on a patch of ice, her leg injury that's healing far too slowly —while she no longer needs her cane, she's still limping and it's humiliating.

They took to one another. Since then, they eat lunch and dinner together with John Paradis, a genuine and loyal client of the bookstore. When he's in Montreal, he comes to browse at least once a month. He's now been travelling since the spring. The West Indies in March, then Paris—he was there at the time of the terrorist attack at Harry's Bar—St. Petersburg, Rome, Venice. They'll certainly see one another again; he plans to return in October or November.

In the biography, there's that passage, very brief, where Columbus meets Beatriz Enriquez in Cordoba, and falls in love with her—at least if he's capable of loving. He fathers her a child who will become his biographer. "This weighs heavy on my heart," he wrote in his journal. These words remain, today still, enigmatic. This what? What did he mean, what did he regret, what weighed upon him? Did he even write to Beatriz when he was on the other side of the world? The biography only mentions his letters to the Catholic Kings. He nevertheless acknowledged the child and that is to his credit.

Beatriz ... She wanted to be Dante's Beatriz, his guide, his muse, and ... No, she doesn't want to think about him anymore, and yet she does. She thinks of him still, after all these months. A thorn in her side. Those walks in hell with him: that is definitely over. It almost cost her life. When you think about it, going out on such a night in the freezing rain to meet that ... ascetic, that scrawny tea drinker—she didn't even dare order a glass of wine in his presence—that scarecrow, that Dante-obsessed hack—who wanted to rewrite his *Divine Comedy*, no less. Then finding him in that hideout of taxi drivers, that pathetic restaurant in La Petite-Patrie. As if it were possible to find the end of the world in La Petite-Patrie! How could she not have understood at the first date, at Café Dante that time, of course, that she was dealing with a fanatic, that nothing good would come of it? Although, a scarecrow—she's exaggerating. He had a certain elegance. She almost thought herself in love with him, truth be told; she was almost, would have been had he given her the slightest encouragement. And a hack:

she's being unfair. She has never read a single line of his. The man was and has remained a mystery.

Gone too are the classified ads in the Saturday paper —that's how she and Dante found one another. "Writer seeking female collaborator." Something like that. Terse. No, it wasn't "writer," just "seeking," "Seeking female reader for collaboration." And she, already won over. She saw herself discussing literature with a scholar. Or founding a reading club, fans of *In Search of Lost Time*, and spending evenings exchanging profound thoughts around a pot of linden tea, a tray of madeleines that she would have learned to bake. It was nothing like that.

It was this personal ad, and it alone, to which she replied. Before, she merely read them, giggling alone, softly. Besides, it's dangerous to reply to personal ads. Isn't that how the awful Landru recruited his victims? And personal ads in newspapers are tacky: people now seek their partners online.

She was never his ghostwriter, no, she assisted him in his quest, that was all. But it was rather twisted. He asked her to look in newspapers, on the Internet, for crimes and atrocities of the twentieth and twenty-first centuries, to list the dictators, assassins, and other psychopaths. He took charge of inventing punishments for new sins. But there are no new sins. They've all been committed since the first fratricide: people only reproduce them, endlessly. A few old sins punished by the genuine Dante— adultery, sodomy—now are no more, fortunately, except in some countries.

Béatrice and Dante. The poet and his muse wandering through the seven circles of the cursed place. The image had seduced her. For her, the game turned out badly.

Here is what happened: she slipped on a piece of black ice as she was heading excitedly to their weekly meeting. A few steps away from the End of the World, almost there. Multiple fractures of the kneecap, torn ligament. Collapsed in an oily puddle, unable to stand up. A passer-by saw her, dialed 911, then the ambulance arrived. She wanted to tell him she was quitting; she couldn't take hell and its damned anymore. Or, if he'd agree, she'd be interested in paradise, concentrating her research on the artists, researchers, patrons, and other philanthropists: they exist, fortunately. Sometimes she wonders if the fall was a punishment, without knowing what her misdeed was.

She still limps like Lola in the old movie, and it's been six months: it happened one March evening, on the spring solstice—but in Montreal, does spring exist? In Montreal, spring is a word, nothing more, a date on the calendar. And the beautiful floral umbrella, lost in the slush. Strangely, she feels as if she misses the umbrella more than anything else. It was pink, with daisies that she'd sewn patiently all around to brighten up the greyness. That evening, she was using it for the first time.

Yet ... how does the saying go? Out of bad comes good? To recover, as it were, recover her balance, her zest for life, she spent two weeks on Paradise Island in June, and there ... A kind of miracle. She met Max, a Czech private detective whose surname had more consonants than vowels. She was not expecting it; expected nothing, in fact. They celebrated one evening on a pirate ship, the *Queen of the Sea*. Drank champagne, danced, not too much due to her handicap, just the slow dances. And afterwards ... They did it again the next day and the day after. He was gentle and warm, walked at her pace—very slowly—holding her elbow, and for a few days, she almost forgot her crippled leg. Then, well, then each of them boarded their planes.

He lives in Prague. They wrote one another, still write, weekly emails in their poor English.

She'll check if she received a message from him, but first wants to find the title of the book they spoke of earlier. The story took place in Rome. Here it is: *In the Cauldron of the Borgias*. There was, she remembers, a wide variety of fish in the dishes. Entertaining, rather convincing, well documented. She noted that Rodrigo Borgia was elected pope in 1492, the year America was discovered; it struck her that he took the name of Alexander VI, that the French chef, one Guillaume Lahire, practiced his art at the Vatican. She gave it two and a half stars.

She is organizing her thoughts, at least trying. Three men occupy them. To begin with, John Paradis. A new chemistry has developed between them during the journey; they're on the same wavelength. At the bookstore, he would greet her courteously, exchange trivial remarks with her. Now they talk a lot together, laugh, sometimes even—a bit, not meanly—at Marjolaine: she's so naïve, like earlier, at lunch, that stuff about cannibals. The poor woman was offended. But Béatrice only has to see how JP looks at the mysterious woman always in black to understand that she's not the chosen one. What about Max? He's at the other end of the world. Dante. Yes, Dante, still him. The thorn in her side.

Good, there's a message from Max in her inbox. She reads it, not sure she understands everything, seeks words with which to respond, but now the little Englishman, the novelist's companion, bursts into the library, interrupting her daydream. He seems unwell.

"You not feel good?" asks Béatrice, alarmed.

He does not answer. He appears to be on the verge of tears.

He sits down, or rather lets himself sink into a chair and remains there, a faraway look in his eyes, seeming lost, overwhelmed.

"You want see the doctor?"

There is a nurse on the ship. The Englishman is perhaps seasick. Yet the sea is very calm today. How do you say *mal de mer* in English?

"You sick sea?"

He shakes his head. But why does he remain silent?

"Life isn't fair," he stammers in a husky voice.

Beatrice understands, but doesn't know what to reply. Life isn't fair? Of course it isn't, what did he think? It is not, nor has it ever been. Her torn ligament is proof of that. Justice is but a word, like spring.

"Rudolf, Maximilian, Pushkin: all betrayed."

"Be what?"

The word he said—jabbered—Béatrice does not understand. Why did she refuse to learn English when she had the opportunity? She has to look for the translation on her laptop, but doesn't know how to spell the word.

"How you write?" she wants to ask.

But he is not listening.

"All betrayed," he repeats, louder this time.

She still does not understand. With these cryptic words, he stands up and leaves.

8

Evening in Puerto Vallarta

*Did they not know that the horizon
recedes as one moves forward,
that you never reach it?*

*A terse postcard from Paradise Island, the one
with three coconut trees, last May, to
say she was still alive, that she was fine.*

They celebrated one evening on a pirate ship, the
Queen of the Sea.

SHE LEFT PARADISE Island in July. Her contract ended; she would no longer play the pirate—Blood Mary—on the *Queen of the Sea*. She returned incognito to Montreal. She didn't have the heart to see her family. Her adoptive family. To hear her mother whine in her three and a half on Boulevard Pie-IX: "You're never in touch. Where were you, Daphné? Where is that, Paradise Island? You have no heart, Daphné." Or: "Why, Daphné? Why did you do that?" *But you said it, Mother; it's because I have no heart—I never had one.* As for her father, she preferred, prefers not to think about it.

One day, on Paradise Island, she felt like going out to the end of the ocean, to sink into its salty sweetness, its power, its violence, let herself be swallowed up. It was tempting, almost irresistible: she nearly gave in to the call of nothingness. Silence, oblivion. She swam toward infinity, the horizon that recedes as you move forward. Then she thought of the sharks, the sharp teeth on her skin, and returned to the shore.

When she lied on the TV reality show, when she said her adoptive father had sexually abused her in her childhood, and she cried—real tears—she knew that he was in bad shape. He'd lost his daughter Fanny in Florida three months earlier. The apple of his eye, born of his sperm, his blood, his genuine daughter, Fanny. It was like hitting a man already down. That's what she can't forgive herself for; that's why she was swimming.

If she lied, it was because she was blinded by the desire to take home the jackpot: one hundred thousand dollars, tax exempt: nothing else mattered. She wanted to go to China so badly, the China of her birth. That's why she lied, why she cried. It had nothing to do with him. It came out on its own: an impulse, just a story she was telling, without malice or premeditation. But what's done is done, and beating herself will change nothing. She didn't win the jackpot. She won the consolation prize: a week's vacation in a place they called Lady Rose, on Paradise Island, where she stayed three months. Hired, when she ran short of money, to entertain vacationers in her pirate costume. Life, she knows, is a series of passages: to survive, you have to be able to turn the page.

She returned to Montreal, and once there, went back to dance at the Geisha Bar. She didn't know how to do anything else to earn money fast. But she relinquished her former disguise: blonde hair, cowboy hat, pistol, and lasso. Usually girls just undulated following the music more or less, taking sensual poses, head tilted back, twisting and swaying their hips, wrapping themselves around a pole while feigning orgasm—that's all that's expected from the performance. Daphné had always wanted roles to play, characters to portray. That was the key to her success at the Geisha Bar; they all asked for the Chinese blonde in her Far West number. In high school, she belonged to the drama group; people thought she had talent. She especially liked Shakespeare; Iago was her favourite character. Iago, the traitor in *Othello*. Not for his treacherousness, no, because of his line: *I am not what I am.* She said it too. *I am not Daphné Laframboise. I was born in Shanghai; I am Chinese. My name, my real name, is Raspberry Perfume. I am not what I am.* She repeated that line in her head, in every possible way. It was a male part; she did not play it at the end of the year show—they always staged a Shakespeare play. Nor did she play the blonde and slender Ophelia, or Desdemona or Juliet: she didn't have the physique for the job. Only the servant roles, and then, in her last year, she finally portrayed her first lead: she was Katherina, the bad-tempered girl in *The Taming of the Shrew.*

She did not persevere. Jobs are too rare for girls with her physique. At the end of high school, she abandoned her studies and worked in one shop then another. At eighteen, she had her hair dyed blonde and became a nude dancer. Her adoptive parents never knew. Her father thought she was in a ballet jazz company: it gave her a good laugh.

≈ Yes, before, it was the Far West. This time, she prepared two numbers. In the first, the day number, she was disguised as a fake geisha: the boss had insisted. In Chinatown she bought a long—synthetic—silk dress, turquoise with fifty-one mother-of-pearl buttons—plastic, in reality, but very good imitations—that she unbuttoned one by one, very slowly, before appearing nude as the day she was born over there in Shanghai, all body hair completely removed. In the evenings, wearing a white blouse and black skirt, she undressed to the theme song of an old movie, *Broken Wings*, sung in French by another Daphné, a Frenchwoman with blue hair. She'd found the film on YouTube, and watched it three times in a row. At the end, like Lola in the film, she wrote on a mirror the words *Forgive me*.

When she earned enough money—three weeks was enough; she danced afternoons and evenings without taking one day off—she bought an air ticket for Puerto Vallarta, a destination chosen by chance, her index finger pointed on a map of Mexico, eyes closed. She rented an apartment for two months on Airbnb. That's where she now lives.

She met Luis the first week; it all happened very simply. He was selling silver jewellery on the beach. She bought a ring from him, then, the next day, suggested that she sell them with him. They'd make a team, share the profits. At first, he wouldn't hear of it. She ended up convincing him. "I speak better English than you," she said. "I can be firm with the tourists; I'm an expert in seduction. And I know how to command respect."

Luis' family lives in Mexico: a wife, three children. His eldest son is called Paco, like the grandfather who died in the earthquake. Paquito. Cuauhtémoc is the young-est, still a baby. In the afternoon, after school, equipped with a rag, Paquito polishes shoes in the subway. Daphné doesn't like to imagine him kneeling at people's feet; she thinks she sees Luis at the same age. He replies that such is life: everyone has to pull together. His wife works as a cleaner. He visits them one weekend a month. The rest of the time, Daphné has him to herself.

They won't have children together. He doesn't want any more; she doesn't want any. She wouldn't be a good mother; she doesn't have the maternal instinct, never had a model. The first one, the Chinese woman, abandoned her when she was a baby. And the other one, the Québé-coise woman, no point in discussing. Not that she was mean to her. No. But always with her nose in a novel, caught up in her sentimental dreams, always with a tear in her eye, soft and spineless, not someone you want to imitate.

There is no longer that rage in her like before, the rage that haunted her, guiding her every gesture when she fought with her plastic sword, dressed up as a pirate on the *Queen of the Sea* and each of her steps when she danced at the Geisha Bar.

In the daytime, they walk up and down the beach with their jewellery. Luis admits that business is better with her. He is bringing back more money to his family in Mexico City. She just hopes that he'll bring in enough one day so that Paquito no longer will have to get down on his knees in the subway. It is always sunny. They eat tacos, tortillas, avocados, mangos; she who used to bare-ly eat has become fond of food. They drink, he his cer-veza, she bottled water—she doesn't want to get sick.

They gave each other pet names: she calls him Lou, he, Nena. In the evening, after they've polished the silver rings and bracelets—he made one especially for her—she prepares jasmine tea. She found a Chinese teapot in the market; porcelain cups without handles, tiny, very delicate, decorated with blue birds. She teaches him words in French; he teaches her words in Spanish. She takes notes; she learns quickly. In Montreal she studied Mandarin, which is much more difficult. She would almost say she's happy if only she knew what the word meant—in French, in Spanish, in Mandarin. She contents herself by saying she is at peace. She does not think of the future, or of the past; she lives in the moment. Each day, she promises herself to send a postcard to her adoptive mother, another beach, other palm trees. The words, however, would be the same: I'm alive and all is well. She also imagines sending one to her father, but doesn't know what she should write: Forgive me, I'm sorry, I didn't want, forgive me. She waits to find the right words.

Luis tells her about the history of Mexico, Cuauhtémoc, Moctezuma, when Mexico was called Tenochtitlan, when people worshipped Quetzalcóatl, the snake with feathers, then the arrival of the conquerors with their horses and their armour.

"And their God," Daphné said.

"Their God."

His face darkens.

"Ours weren't any better."

Yet he is a believer, wears a gold chain around his neck with a medal of the Virgin. He exclaims *Madre de Dios*, often makes the sign of the cross.

He asks her to tell him her own story, but she is

ashamed; she doesn't want to. She replies that she had no past before him, that she has no story. Everyone has one, he insists. She says that her own is too ordinary; isn't worth being told.

When they make love, there isn't much foreplay. Almost always in the same position. They never say they love one another.

Life is lighter, yes, life is now light. It's as if the sad weight she's always carried on her shoulders has been removed, her birth as an outcast. She thinks she has never before known this lightness, this tenderness. She feels unburdened, new, washed, empowered, calmed. Forgiven.

She doesn't know if she'll spend her entire life like this. Perhaps not. Now she is well. "*Carpe diem*, Daphné," she repeats to herself. "Live in the moment."

She wants him to talk to her about Malinche and Hernando Cortés, for him to tell her, again and again, what Cuauhtémoc said while the soles of his feet were being burned. "And me, do you think I am lying on a bed or roses?" She imagines the pain, imagines the courage. Did he really say that? Luis assures her that he did.

"So there used to be roses in Mexico?"

Luis shrugs his shoulders.

"It's an image, Nena. But why not roses? We have so many flowers here."

Some people think he actually said: "Am I enjoying some kind of delight or bath?" How to know? He spoke in his language, Nahuatl. It was the Spanish who translated it; it is their translation that went down in history. But Daphné says no, it was Malinche—was she even familiar with roses? Don't look any farther, Nena. The Spanish interpreted Malinche, that's all. Cuauhtémoc simply wanted to say that having your feet in boiling oil hurts.

His son Paquito prefers the bed of roses. So does she.

He says that she is like Paquito, who always wants to be told the same thing, the life of the last Aztec Emperor, Cuauhtémoc, the Descending Eagle. Or the setting sun, depending on the interpretation given to it—the eagle was the symbol of the sun in Aztec culture. Paquito likes resistance, the unwillingness to speak, even in torture, to reveal where the gold was hidden. He likes his life, but the death of the Eagle always makes him cry. Cortés hanged from a tree, a death unworthy of a hero such as he.

A fine monument to him has been erected at the intersection of Avenida de los Insurgentes and Paseo de la Reforma in Mexico City. "You'll see it when you come to the big city, Nena." That is how history strives to repair its mistakes. A monument, a face on a postage stamp. A name engraved on a tombstone.

Luis says that this death marked the end of the empire. The Eagle had fallen. "But Mexico was born. Countries are born like us in blood and tears." Daphné thinks of her own birth in China, blood on a white sheet, her mother's tears upon seeing she'd given birth to a daughter. In Paradise Island, when she swam, it was also that image that she wanted to drown.

She will not have children.

≈ Usually, it's like that. Jewellery on the beach, stories and tea, love without foreplay, unadorned. But this evening, this evening she is crying, and nothing can console her. She's just read the news on her tablet. What remained of Fanny discovered in Savannah, Georgia. *Sweet Georgia*

—she has already danced to that song, her lasso whirling in the air, boot heels clicking. Waves of guilt rush over her now. She had nothing to do with it, but feels responsible. For what? She doesn't know. Responsible, guilty for never having loved her. Her half-sister, her younger adoptive sister, Fanny. We think the past is dead and buried, think we are freed from it, and suddenly it rises up, submerging us, like a tsunami, taking away everything, the blue birds on the teapot, kind words, jewellery, the peace we thought we'd finally found. How could she have loved her, obsessed as she was with her Chinese dream, and filled with rancour for that fake father who purred like a big cat in his house in Outremont with his wife, the psychologist, and their new children? Whether she loved Fanny or not would not have changed any of that, yet she can't help crying. The ogre and the wolf that so fascinated her in fairy tales ended up devouring the child. In watered-down versions, the children were saved. She never believed that. She has known Fanny's fate since learning of her disappearance last December: she never had any hopes or illusions. It's just that now, seeing the words written on the screen of her tablet, it has become final.

In the face of her tears, Luis is distraught. He doesn't understand, wonders if it's his fault, what he did to hurt her. He's never seen her cry. He pours her some cold tea, caresses her hair, her hand, her knee, her face.

"¿ Porque lloras asi, Nena ? ¿Porque lloras ? ¿ Que te pasa ?"

She cannot answer. She shakes her head.

"Nada. Nada."

9

The *End of the World*, Afternoon

*The couple lost their daughter in Florida
last winter.*

*What do you say? My condolences?
My sympathies?*

Sofia Perovskaïa, a hard-line anarchist.

FLORENCE, ROBERT, JONATHAN. The mother, her husband, her brother. The ship's sad trio.

She, in the small lounge, where the other day Marjolaine had surprised the tattooed couple in the heat of action. Alone now — or with her ghosts. The child that she was, the rebellious teenager, and then, later, at nineteen, passionately in love with a married man, who left his wife and their adopted daughter, a little Chinese girl, for her. The first time, the ghost was hitchhiking at the entrance to the highway. Where was it going? I was going anywhere, on an adventure, nowhere, as they say. I was going nowhere and he stopped, very gently so gently, I got into his car, a metallic grey BMW. I've forgotten nothing — it was summer, the slightly tart, musky scent of his aftershave, the music playing in the car. Nor had she forgotten the theme song of a tacky movie, *Broken Wings*; that song was so sad. He said he adored it; he was a movie buff. The movie was screened sometimes at the cinematheque, but at nineteen she wasn't interested in old movies. Then she saw it with him; he brought over the DVD. He had a collection of repertory films: Renoir, *L'Atalante* by Jean Vigo, Fritz Lang, Bob Elkis, Orson Welles, all in black and white. Even the famous *Battleship Potemkin* with the baby in its carriage rolling down the steps; the sailors had found worms in their meat, they rebelled—she shuddered when he told her. When they watched *Broken Wings*, that evening, she especially liked the scene where Lola limps in the night, her heel broken, the black mass of ships swaying in the port, in Southampton, likes beasts lying in wait. For him, it was the end that was moving, the words that Lola writes with her lipstick on the mirror: *Forgive me*—really too poignant, that scene. Then she became pregnant with Fanny, and he left the other two. She was twenty; Robert was fifteen years older. And then Fanny was born, her adorable, adored daughter.

The ghosts turn and jostle one another; they shout in her head. "You're not a ghost," she says to Fanny. "Not a ghost. Where are you? You're somewhere, I know, you're alive, I know you're alive. I gave you life; you can't not live, you can't die, not die before me." Inside her, something grows, something takes hold, something no longer grows, takes hold despite everything. It has been like that since the first instant or almost, when she stopped seeing Fanny by the pool, a voice whispered in her ear: "It's over."

She has lost her adorable daughter, her adored daughter; that's the ghost that shouts the loudest, it's the most passionate. The one that refuses to be silent. "Mommy."

Day and night. Sometimes it shouts at the top of its lungs, sometimes it moans, cries, sobs, groans, pants; it never shuts up. "Mommy! I'm afraid, Mommy!" It calls out to her from the bottom of ... what?

"You're not a ghost," she says again and again. "Not you." But she's thinking of Cathy, in *Wuthering Heights*, the ghost that called to Heathcliff, at night, who moaned constantly at his window, every night. She, too, has a ghost that moans, and Heathcliff, tormented, could no longer sleep. She can't sleep either, except when she takes a sleeping pill, and when she takes one, sleep sweeps down over her like a cat on its prey. She imagines the big cat, sees it, its spotted coat: a lynx or a panther — Fanny's favourite character in the TV series. Her sleep does not bring her rest. Her sleep is haunted; blood squirts everywhere, shouting is heard. Fanny struggles in the claws of a monster: she sees her, but cannot reach her. Her dreams are haunted; she exhausts herself following Fanny whom the monster carries farther away, always farther, like the horizon that recedes as you move forward. It's worse when she's asleep; she doesn't want to sleep anymore.

Fanny had devoured the novel. And she, Florence, understood that her daughter was in love with the rebel; she understood why. I too, she says, loved Heathcliff. I was your age; I too dreamed of being carried away. He carried me away on his horse; he and I galloped on the moors, in the night, our capes floating in the wind. Girls all have the same dreams. The dreams of Emily Brontë when, alone and sad on her moor, she invented Heathcliff and Cathy. The novel ends well — does it end well? She no longer remembers how it ends. Cathy is dead, but does Heathcliff die at the end? It's vague; she no longer remembers the book's ending, but she's angry at Emily Brontë for having Cathy die. They discussed it, however, for hours, she and Fanny, when she read it. Fanny could talk about it forever; it was last fall. Time goes by so quickly, but life is so slow; there's a poem like that—how slow life seems, and how violent the hope of love. Those are perhaps the last words; she forgets if that's how the poem ends; she can't even remember who wrote it.

This cruise was not a good idea; she can't wait for it to end. Only two more interminable days; she regrets having given in. It was Jonathan's idea. Jonathan pushed and pushed. The Aegean, islands filled with myths and history: Crete, Santorini, Mykonos. And a ship called *End of the World*. She thought that those myths were cruel— wasn't there a monster in Knossos, the Minotaur, that devoured children? You need to take a break from your worries, have a change of scenery, Jonathan said. Strange expression. Will taking a break make them go away? It hurts no matter where you are. She gave in, but the worries have not gone away.

It happened last December, nine months ago, already; enough time to make a child, when you think of it. The disappearance—the runaway, kidnapping, abduction, whatever name you give it. The event—that word seems less tragic. So, the event. In December, the day of the solstice—today is the autumn equinox. Time goes by so quickly, but life is so slow; the days are so long, and how violent, hope.

And what were you doing when Fanny vanished, interrupts the ghost in her head, the woman who she was nine months ago, carefree and cheerful on the balcony in the sun in St. Petersburg, Florida, happy to escape the snow and cold that remained at home. Three children at the pool, down below. Fanny, lying face down on her towel, reading *Lolita*, headphones on her ears. She was listening to Daphné sing, for sure, her idol for two months. The singer with the blue hair singing *Broken Wings*— the song from the old movie. The first time they made love, she and Robert, when they conceived Fanny, was after seeing that movie. Do you tell that to your daughter —does a daughter want to imagine her parents making love in bed, a teenager who no doubt is experiencing her first sensual feelings? She didn't say anything. Fanny listened—listens?—to it constantly, young people are like that: insatiable, obsessive. The two boys had quarrelled; now they were playing cards, and I was thinking of the menu for Christmas. The capon, because a turkey is too much when you're only five; afterwards you have to eat the leftovers for a week in soup, in sandwiches, au gratin: you're fed up. So the capon, green peas, and, and ... she is searching, no longer knows what she wanted to serve for Christmas Eve, or Christmas dinner; she no longer knows if it was for Christmas Eve or Christmas dinner. A capon, peas, and what else? Oh. Yes, the log, of course, the ... chestnut log, no, the kids wouldn't like that, so chocolate, vanilla, strawberry ... coffee, yes, she's sure of it, she was thinking of buying a coffee-flavoured log. There was that French bakery, not far away; her mother had ordered a mocha log for Christmas Eve there the year before; the children had loved it, even Fanny had taken seconds. Fanny would refuse to eat the capon; for some time she's been vegetarian; so she must have been thinking of something for Fanny. A vegetarian dish just for her vegetarian daughter, was she thinking of that?

What had she planned? She can't remember. And for the first course, surely something refined, she forgets what it was, something light, soup perhaps, vichyssoise. Or salad? Italian—tomato, bocconcini, and basil? Moroccan—oranges and black olives? She was like that on the balcony, carefree, thinking about dishes for Christmas Eve or Christmas dinner, weighing the pros and cons, soup, salad, while her children, below ... But she knows that she was reading. I was reading about the history of Czarist Russia, Sofia Perovskaïa, a hardline anarchist, who was hung with her accomplices in St. Petersburg for the murder of Alexander II or III—I can't remember which, or was it a Nicholas? No, Nicholas II was executed elsewhere with his family, so it was Alexander II or III. A bomb under his train. Or his carriage, I can't remember. His son built a church on the site of the tragedy: The Savior on Spilled Blood, a cathedral. She has seen photos with the domes, the colours, the icons: so it was not a train, it was a carriage. The bomb under the train was another time, another Czar. I was thinking of St. Petersburg, Russia; I wanted to go there with Robert in summer, this summer, without the children. I was planning that trip in my head, to finally see the white nights, an old dream, an adolescent fantasy: the white nights of St. Petersburg. Dostoevsky wrote a book called something like that; I read it long ago and ever since I've dreamed of the white nights. I wanted the music of the balalaikas, the folklore. I wanted the midnight sun, vodka, caviar, blinis, gypsies, and boats on the Neva: an old dream I wanted to finally fulfil. That's it: I was dreaming on the balcony.

But why were you reading, dreaming on the balcony?

You could have, should have been reading and dreaming at the pool with your children. You'd have been near them, near her; you were reading, dreaming, instead of watching your children. That day, you were not a good mother, you weren't watchful, you preferred your dreams, your whims, you'd have seen her disappear, you'd have caught her, you ... The ghost speaks angrily; filled with reproach. He doesn't want to forgive her for remaining on the balcony, carefree and dreamy, while below the tragedy played out. No, she says, no. She wants to justify herself. No, it wouldn't have changed anything. Fanny had decided to leave; it was her choice. She would have said, I don't know, that she was going to the bathroom. She would have taken her beach bag; I couldn't have followed her—you don't follow a girl who is twelve, almost thirteen, step by step. She would have been thirteen on May 3. I made a cake that evening. The two boys blew out the candles; no one ate it. I spent the night crying; the next morning I threw it in the garbage. But perhaps while you were reading, dreaming, perhaps a predator spotted her. She was, she is so pretty; perhaps he lured her on some pretext, and then ... No, she says. No, Fanny wanted to leave, she'd planned to run away. She stole money from her father, two or three hundred American dollars, a lot of money, while my back was turned. I was squeezing oranges; she'd planned everything. I trusted her and she betrayed me; she put everything she needed in her beach bag: money, tampons, jeans, a sweater, a change of underwear. She just forgot *Lolita* beside the pool; it wouldn't have mattered if I were there. But maybe yes. You should have seen it when she went down to the pool, sullen, uncommunicative: you should have read it in the impenetrable look in her eyes, should have understood what she was plotting. You chose to read and dream on the balcony.

"Stop beating yourself up," Jonathan says to her. She also says it to herself, said it to the women who consult her, consulted her—she is, was a psychologist at the women's prison. She doesn't say it, won't say it anymore: she has been on sick leave since the event. She will not return there, won't help anyone anymore, will never say "Stop beating yourself, turn the page," because she now knows that you don't turn the page. The book remains open at the same page, always, and you always reread the same passage, the same sentence. You know it by heart, and yet you reread it, again and again, you can't stop yourself, you keep on seeking the hidden meaning.

≈ Robert paces back and forth along the deck. He who always stood so straight is now bent. He stops, leans over the rail, eyes staring at the blue sea, the horizon that recedes. Other ships sail along the Aegean Sea; they stop off at the islands, passengers disembark, lighthearted. They buy souvenirs, lighters, T-shirts, fridge magnets, bracelets. He too left the ship, but his heart was heavy, and it was as if he'd seen nothing. Eyes staring at the blue water, he now sees Fanny floating on the waves, Fanny sinking then coming back up, sinking then ... She undulates to the rhythm of the waves; her hair is seaweed; her body is so light. Like the other happy years, before the event, when she looked forward to spending Christmas in Florida, when she jumped in the waves, shouting "Look at me!" Her happy cry. "Look at me, I'm floating, I know how to swim, Daddy!" She refused to use the lifebelt.

"I'm a mermaid, Daddy, look at me!" He rubs his eyes. The mermaid is no longer there. He rubs his eyes. "Come back," he says. "Come back, I'm watching you." She is no longer there.

Fanny did not want to go to Florida this year. Florence reproached herself so much for forcing her. She had activities planned with her friends: it's so important to have friends at her age. Three days of skiing, an end-of-the year party at Melissa's. But do you leave your twelve-year-old daughter—thirteen in the spring—in Montreal, even with friends? They in turn point blame at one another: "It's because of you," "No, it's your fault; you were reading your book on the balcony while she ran away." And Florence, full of rancour: "And you were playing golf instead of taking care of the children." It's true; for some years now he'd developed a passion for golf; futile hours on the green with his clubs and balls. They reproach one another, accuse one another. Yet he still loves, continues to love her; it is she who has rejected him since the event, as if he were guilty. "You confiscated her cell phone; she couldn't call me for help. She would have called me." He knew her; she'd have spent hours on the telephone with her friends in Montreal and the Laurentians, sending texts. It would have cost him a fortune. He told himself that in Florida with her family she wouldn't need it. "She was afraid of you; that's why she left," she said. "Afraid of me? I never touched her." That was before Daphné and her lies. Because after the lies he thought he saw suspicion in Florence's eyes. "Never touched her," he says.

And then there was the theft; he noticed it when he returned from golf, after a drink on the balcony. Three hundred US dollars; he'd have to act harshly when Fanny returned, otherwise what example would he be setting for her two little brothers if she stole with impunity? He'd have to find a punishment to match the crime, deprive her of ... what? Dessert? She couldn't care less; she was no longer five years old. TV—her favourite program, the jaguar, puma, cougar, panther, some sort of wildcat, regardless of the name. Force her to ... eat her meat? She said she was vegetarian: faced with a chicken wing, she'd become indignant, her face contorted: "I'm not a cannibal!" Confiscate her ... the iPod that Florence was going to give her for Christmas—she'd be so happy, in heaven, he could already see her smile, eyes shiny—this year, no gift for you, my daughter. Today, looking at the blue sea, he is angry at himself for even having thought it. *Come back, Fanny; you'll have your iPod, everything you want. I'll give you back your cell phone. Come back, Fanny, I'm looking at you.*

And Fanny vanished. Where? A trace of her was found in a McDonald's on the highway. The server remembered her when he saw the photo: pretty, very thin, wearing a turquoise T-shirt. She spoke bad English, with an accent. She'd ordered a chocolate milkshake. Then a man came to talk to her. The trail stops there: a chocolate milkshake, a man in black. Perhaps she left with him; the server thinks so. She followed him, but there were a lot of people, it was rush hour. He wasn't sure anymore, could not swear to it. He just remembered seeing them for a second at the same table: a man in black, but he didn't look dangerous, leaning toward the girl with the long hair in the turquoise T-shirt. Two cashes down, the girl who'd served the man in black remembered that he ordered a tea, because tea is unusual here; he didn't order anything to eat. He wore a hat, like you see in old movies. Robert thought of the fedora worn by Lola's lover in *Broken Wings*. As for witnesses: how to find them in a place like that? People come and go, they pay cash, swallow their burgers and then leave. Even the security camera revealed nothing. It showed Fanny leave, but the man turned his head away, his hat tilted over his face. The pimply server, not very bright, was therefore the last to have seen her—alive. And the case was closed: so many young people ran away, disappeared into nature; there was a lack of clues, a lost cause, case closed.

Since February, Robert has been part of a group of parents of missing children. A support group; they counsel you in terms of processes, offer a kind of comfort, an attentive ear, a hand on your shoulder. Other parents have lived through it, are living through it. Will live through it, alas. Children have gone missing since the world began, as if sucked up by nothingness, fallen into the void at the end of the horizon. Some are found; there are stories, even after nine months some are found, even after years. It has happened; don't lose hope. Someone is holding her hostage; it's impossible otherwise; she would have returned, repentant perhaps, certainly arrogant, but she would have returned. He doesn't lose confidence, refuses to give up.

He visited the sites of pedophiles, believed—almost hoped—sometimes that he recognized her, a gesture, an attitude, the colour of her hair: was it really her? They must put make up on them; dye the brunettes blonde, the blondes red. Apparently there are specialized places, brothels reserved for perverts like that Humbert—she was reading *Lolita* the day of ... of the event. He hadn't known that.

Mediums, astrologists, fortune-tellers: they all had something to tell, their services to propose. Perhaps some were sincere. People in the group warned him. Most are charlatans, be wary. They only want your money; most of them are vultures. He believed that, though for a while he'd consulted a clairvoyant. She'd seen Fanny in Trois-Rivières. He went there; entered bars, cafés, massage parlours; he even hired a private detective to look for her. One medium spoke of a bearded man; another saw a man whose name began with B; another spoke of a ship, of a faraway country—he saw islands. So, when Jonathan suggested this cruise, Robert thought that *End of the World* was a prophetic name. He went aboard; left the ship at all the stops, scrutinized passengers looking for the slightest clue. The people in the group were right; none of that led to anything. After that milkshake on a Florida highway, Fanny had vanished.

Nevertheless, since the scandal of Daphné on TV, people look at him strangely. Even afterwards, when the liar admitted to having lied. A nude dancer in bars that are called Geisha or possibly Floozie's, and he who thought she was in a dancer in a jazz or ballet company. She won a prize for her slander: a week in a five-star hotel on Paradise Island, a consolation prize, whereas he remains forever inconsolable.

Yes, doubt persists, the spot remains, indelible, like the blood on Lady Macbeth's hands; people look at him strangely, and even though he is guilty of nothing, when they look at him like that he is ashamed.

≈ Jonathan is at the bar; he orders a bottle of rosé wine. He knows where Florence is, in the small lounge; she must be daydreaming, beating herself up, going over all the moments in her head since the one when she was reading a book on Russia at the time of Alexander II. She's been doing that for nine months. Despite his repeating to her that she is not responsible, not guilty, that Fanny had planned her runaway, she claims she hadn't been watchful enough. "I closed my eyes," she says, "closed my eyes when I needed to look." She scarcely eats, doesn't sleep, or when she does, says she slept poorly. "I had bad dreams," she says.

It is he who convinced them to go on this cruise; ten days to ... when he said have a change of scenery, Florence shrugged her shoulders; the hurt would still be there. So he said to get your health back. Or else so you can reconcile. They've been living separately since the event; they scarcely speak to one another when Robert comes to pick up their other children, Jon and Balthazar. They each retreat into their grief, refusing to share it; each blames the other, each believes they are suffering more than the other. Robert—Jonathan pities him—is like a zombie, even more so since his daughter Daphné —he'd always found her shifty—slandered him.

He convinced them to leave the two boys with the grandparents; made them promise to forget their cellphones and laptops, told them he would handle it. He'd keep their telephones and inform them of the news, whatever it was. Just a rest, a bubble outside of time—you need one. The truth is that he thought there wouldn't be any news. It's been nine months since the event—Florence insists on saying event—occurred and there has never been any, except to give false hope. Fanny was spotted here or there, in North or South Carolina, in Georgia, in Virginia, alone, in the company of a redheaded woman, of a man in black. Even in Quebec, someone was sure they recognized her at the border, and as far away as Trois-Rivières—what was she doing in Trois-Rivières?

Now he knows they've found the girl; he learned that yesterday when he answered Florence's phone. Then his mother called in tears, and this morning when, like every morning, he checked the Internet, it was written in black and white on his screen. Yesterday he said nothing, today neither; he's afraid to speak of it, doesn't know how to inform them, and he a translator by profession, is short of words, wants to let the trip draw to a close—they'll find out soon enough. He doesn't know much; he doesn't have the details. But what he does know, he'd prefer not to. The body was found in Savannah, Georgia, yesterday afternoon. Near her, the murderer had left the beach bag with what she'd placed inside, the money stolen from her father—less the price of the chocolate milkshake, and her health insurance card: that's how they were able to identify her. She had suffered abuse, sexual and other; her body—what remains of it—shows signs of torture. He thinks of the last book he translated this summer, *Goddess in Gehenna*: he couldn't find a title in French, still hasn't found one. A dreary detective novel, a story about a network of pedophiles: there he couldn't find the words either.

He does not want to be the messenger.

Florence suspects as much, he thinks; something inside her knows it; she doesn't need a telephone, computer or tablet. This morning, she was still more nervous than usual; at noon she didn't want to go to the dining room. He and Robert had a sandwich at the bar while she nibbled on three olives, drinking rosé wine. She had been drinking more since the event. Always parched; she always wants wine. Gin, vodka, whisky. She trembles when she takes her glass. She has started smoking again.

He takes the bottle and the two glasses; he goes to see her. He will know what to say when he is next to her: platitudes. I do not want to be the messenger.

He is about to enter the small lounge when that woman suddenly appears. He knows who it is: the cook from the End of the World—not the ship, a restaurant in his neighbourhood that closed this summer, for renovations. He went there occasionally when his fridge was empty; often in the wee hours of the morning after spending the night translating reports, cookbooks, thrillers or sentimental novels, he'd be famished. He always ordered the holiday special: turkey, peas, mashed potatoes, cranberry sauce, available twenty-four hours a day every day of the year. Apple pie for dessert, unlimited coffee.

What does she want? What is she looking for? She remains frozen for a microsecond, looking panic-stricken, eyes flitting from left to right, then sees Florence and before he has time to stop her, to tell her to go away, she rushes forward.

"My condolences," she cries out, taking Florence in her arms. "My sympathies."

10

In Cabarete, a Fiancée Conspicuously Absent

Her fiancé was waiting for her in the Dominican Republic;
she was supposed to get married tomorrow morning.

History is not an exact science, fortunately.
Cathy, in Wuthering Heights.

PANDEMONIUM AT THE Gamba Alegre. Outside it's raining, but inside, the celebration will soon begin. The restaurant is decorated with garlands and multicolour balloons; a piñata hangs from the ceiling, and freshly ironed white tablecloths are on the tables. The silver ... well here, it can be more accurately described as stainless steel, but it's gleaming nevertheless.

They are all there: Rafa, Matilda and their children, and Concha, her mother Nieves, her brother Raúl, her sisters, her baby. Uncles, aunts, cousins, friends, their brood, plus the neighbours. Maria Flor, the barmaid from Mar Azul, has taken the day off. All have gathered to welcome Enrique's fiancée, a Québécoise named Dorothée. She is arriving this morning; her plane is supposed to land at Puerto Plata's airport at eight twenty. Quique has gone to fetch her with Ernesto, his cousin, who borrowed a car for the occasion.

The marriage will take place at noon. Dorothée will

147

be tired, of course: she had two stops: one in New York, the other in Miami. They just hope she was able to rest a little on the plane.

Raúl will take the photos. The band—one singer and two musicians—is reserved. They will arrive for the banquet, after the ceremony at the church. Matilda has been cooking all night. The main course will of course be the sancocho—beef, pork, chicken, sausage, but no goat. On that point, Quique was uncompromising: Canadians don't eat it, Mother. Dorothée is very sensitive—they don't want to disgust her on her wedding day. Matilda didn't insist, although she knows that something will be missing from the feast. Everything is simmering now in its sauce of aromatic herbs with cassava, yams, sweet potatoes, squash, and plantains. There will be *tostones*, rice, shrimp with ginger and coconut milk, and conch—when she was last there, in February, Dorothée was crazy about them. Avocados—she says they're a hundred times better than the ones imported from Mexico before ripening that you find over there all year long, guavas and mangos. Rafa prepared the sangria—just this once—Nieves made the cake: four layers covered with white icing, decorated with sugar roses, topped with a couple of newlyweds in plastic, hand in hand.

They will spend their honeymoon here; their room is reserved for a week at the Paraíso Sol. Quique will tour her around the island, then she'll return to Canada. He'll follow her in a few months, once the paperwork is finalized. There will be no delay, no problem; everything will be done according to the rules. Dorothée took care of it, she knows how to proceed. She works at the Department of Immigration, in Ottawa. For Quique, this is an un-hoped-for opportunity.

Just now, Concha and Maria Flor are placing the flowers in vases: there will be one on each table. Concha seems sad despite the prevailing excitement.

"Are you still thinking of him?" Maria Flor whispers.

Him, that is another Québécois who Concha met right here, in Cabarete, last March. John Paradis. Except that he did not return.

Concha inclines her head vaguely: it could mean yes; it could mean no. Maria Flor knows that it's yes.

"It couldn't last. He was far too young for you. And married, possibly."

Concha shrugs her shoulders. Too old, perhaps, married, perhaps as well, although she doubts it: he wore no ring. Divorced, then. In any case, he was very kind, and generous: you can't say the same for all tourists. He never looked at the price of the dishes he ordered at the Gamba Alegre. The most expensive ones, often. Always the best quality of rum. He would say, "Come, eat, Conchitita, have anything you like. You're so thin." He called her Conchitita. And the tips he left. With him, she never pretended. Well, didn't pretend too much, not each time. Before he left, he gave her a silver bracelet set with a turquoise stone. She still has it on her wrist.

"It looks as if it will never be my turn."

"Your turn for what?"

"To marry. It's as if I'll never get married. Today, it's Quique. After, it will be you."

Maria Flor is supposed to marry Raúl, Concha's brother, next winter.

"And what's in store for me?"

"Don't worry, nena. Someone else will come along."

Others always come along, tourists, snowbirds, *pájaros de la nieve, oiseaux de la neige*, as they say, but not a single one stays, not a single one has ever come back for her. Concha wonders why not. She believed, no, she didn't believe, she hoped she'd struck it lucky that time. Another illusion, one more. A tour guide, that's what she says to them when she approaches them. She sells them paintings by her brother Raúl, sends them fishing on her cousin Manolo's boat, brings them to eat at her Uncle Rafa's Gamba, to dance salsa in the evening at Mar azul and drink lots of piña coladas and other rum-based cocktails. She herself only drinks Coke: she has to keep her head on her shoulders. For all that, she receives a commission—naturally.

The extras—there are some—she keeps for herself. And, even tired at the end of the day, you have to have put food on the table. Her father, a fisherman, disappeared into the sea on a stormy night. She is the eldest of the family. Two of her sisters work as chambermaids at the Paraíso Sol. The youngest are still in school.

"And he had such a nice name. Paradis, *Paraíso* . . . My Paquito will never have a father," she concludes, sadly.

Rafa checks his watch. Ten fifteen: the engaged couple will be there soon. Matilda removes her apron. She has put on her prettiest dress, the red one with white polka dots, and fastened her black hair in a bun on her neck. Children run around between the tables, try to catch the balloons, want to break the piñata. They are ordered to sit down and remain quiet.

Although the restaurant is closed for the day, a couple is having their breakfast on the covered patio. It is raining hard—in fact, it's rained all week, a tropical storm named Margot. But since they've been taking all their meals here for the last three days, Rafa doesn't have the heart to send them away. The girl ordered a fruit plate —perhaps she is afraid of gaining weight—the man, heavy-set, the traditional breakfast, *mangú,* scrambled eggs, sausage, cheese, sliced avocado. A bottle of spring water, coffee, *con leche* for her, black for him.

It is nevertheless strange to have chosen Cabarete. But Ivan Cristu—the one they call the bear of the Balkans—doesn't like trendy places. He said that there would be no risk of being followed by the paparazzi here, the jet set wouldn't be interested in Cabarete. Besides, in September, it's still in the middle of the rainy season. So, even fewer tourists. He wanted but one thing: peace.

He is a filmmaker. The pretty girl sitting across from him is called Marjorie Dubois, an actress. They've spent three days developing the female character of his next film, *Noche Triste,* in which she will portray Malinche, the Aztec interpreter of Cortés. For some people, says Cristu, Malinche symbolizes betrayal; others see her as the mother of Mexico. She has been associated with the Llorona, the weeping woman, and even with the Virgin Mary who also weeps. Her only son crucified: who wouldn't cry in her shoes? What he, Ivan Cristu, wants, are nuances. And most of all, no question of seeing her madly in love, obsessed by her love for Hernando Cortés. It has not been proved that she loved him. And the conquistador as a bashful lover is even less likely. He wants an intelligent woman. For she was intelligent, he has no doubt. Exceptionally so, even. He insists: he wants nuances. Was she ambitious? Was she a visionary? Or did she simply want to save her skin? A bit of all of that, according to Cristu.

Perhaps save her people, Marjorie suggested. Ivan shook his head. Besides, what people are you speaking of? An Aztec, she had been sold as a slave to the Mayans, then given as a gift to the Spanish with about twenty girls like her. If it's the Mexicans you are talking about—Aztec, Mayan, Mixtecs or others—they were decimated, reduced to slavery, massacred: twenty-five million inhabitants before the conquest, approximately three million a half century later, hanged, mutilated, burned at the stake. Cristu's *Noche Triste* will have no resemblance to Cortés' *nuit triste* when he and his band almost lost everything. He is more interested in the one who fell upon the Aztec people, and not just them, after the arrival of the Spanish on their land. Her people, whoever they were, Malinche did not save them, Margarita—he calls her Margarita, Margot sometimes, like the storm, for fun. And even Malinche. For him, Marjorie is not a real name.

She knows it; she has also read Todorov. She knows that for him the conquest was a genocide. She's been immersed for three months in the history of Mexico—Cuauhtémoc's feet in boiling oil, the bed of roses. She knows all that by heart, has read the life of Malinche by Laura Esquivel, in Spanish, equipped with a dictionary, and her *Like Water for Chocolate*, in French this time. (The one hundred and seventy eggs in the wedding cake made her feel nauseous, a recipe she will not soon forget.)

She is even learning Nahuatl. But other historians speak of human sacrifices when the Aztecs dominated the territory, thousands of people sacrificed each year, flower wars, describe their empire as the bloodiest one experienced in America. They even see Cortés as a liberator. What does it mean? Where is the truth?

Cristu shrugged his shoulders. You choose your angle, that's all. Or your historian. Not only one truth exists. In the end, there's not much to choose between them.

She said: "I don't believe it."

And he: "When Cortés had enough of her, or when he no longer needed her services, he passed her off to one of his men. But his men wanted to marry women from the Spanish nobility, certainly not Indigenous women. The Indigenous women they raped. The life of Malinche was not worth much." Marjorie thought like he. Life wasn't worth much, at that time. The life of an Indigenous woman. What is more, the life of a girl.

"Is it worth more now?"

"They kidnapped her son, Martín."

"Probably died under torture, in Spain. The times were patriarchal, as you well know."

His disappearance is a mystery, and will remain so. History does not have all the answers. Murdered? Perhaps. By one group or another. Victim of an epidemic. Perhaps again. Perhaps even died as a centenarian in a remote village in Michoacán.

But now they've exhausted the subject. This evening, they will return home, she to Vancouver, he to somewhere in California or Nevada—no one knows where the bear has made his lair.

≈ In the morning, he's always hungry, so he eats: a slice of sausage, a piece of bread, a forkful of scrambled eggs. She pretends to nibble.

She talks about the movie she saw last night on TV, *Sissi*, in Spanish. She talks to him about it, but he's looking at her breasts, small but prominent, almost alert beneath the navy blue sweater, small breasts like those of birds, very round, plump, and quivering. Malinche's must have been like that. Oh! Malinche, Malinche, he sees her: he'd almost say he recognizes her. How old was she when she interpreted for the conqueror, when he slept with her? About twenty, more or less the age of his actress. But his Margot has the same serious gaze as Malinche on the Aztec drawings, eyes that seem to see into the very depths of people's souls. It is for her eyes that he chose her. And me, I am Hernando Cortés, *con mi lengua*—for now he is thinking in Spanish.

"Horribly sentimental," he says between two mouthfuls, and for him, nothing is worse.

She admits it was romanticized. Everything wasn't as rosy as that between the Empress and her husband Franz Joseph. She talks about it, but he's looking at her the way, he thinks, Cortés looked at Malinche when she spoke, making out the breasts quivering like birds beneath the white cotton. Because, he couldn't care less about the moods of the empress.

"Who says that life is rosy, Margarita? Life is red. Or, very often, black."

This morning she is wearing glasses. She is not made up.

"Take them off," he says.

"Why?"

"I want to see Malinche the way people will see her in my movie."

She places them on the table next to the plate she has barely touched.

"At first it was her sister Helene he was supposed to marry," she says. "The Emperor, I mean. Franz Joseph."

So she begins to wonder. For in this case, no Rudolf, so no Mayerling, so no François-Ferdinand as heir to the throne of Austria-Hungary, no assassination at Sarajevo, no First World War, no Second, no Hitler, no Auschwitz, no Israel, no conflict between Israel and Palestine. Perhaps even no terrorist attacks.

"You're rewriting history, Margot."

"I really would like to rewrite it. I'd write it differently."

"Of course. You eliminate wars, genocides, regicides, patricides, everyone is nice, everyone lives happily, heaven on earth until the end of time.

"You wonder if the entire history of the world does not depend on one look, on one desire."

"A passion between Lucy and the Cro-Magnon man?"

The image makes her smile despite herself.

"Love, hatred, jealousy," she says. "We don't care about much. It's depressing. The First World War, eighteen million killed, victims with severe facial injuries, all that. Do you realize?"

"The First World War, the Second would have taken place anyway. Too much tension. Sarajevo was only the spark. The fire was already smouldering. For a long time. You know as well as I. It's still smouldering. Other wars will come."

"The First would have perhaps taken place. But the Second?"

"The Second as well. Now you're thinking gloomy thoughts. It's because of the rain."

"No ... Yes, I am gloomy, but not because of the rain. I'm used to it. In Vancouver, it rains on average a hundred and sixty-six days a year ... The question is: "Are we that much a product of chance?""

He shrugs his shoulders.

"Sissi was less happy that you might believe," she says.

Her again, the neurotic empress. He sniggers.

"The poor thing. Did her satin dress have a snag? Did she lose a diamond from her crown?"

She replies that since he is speaking of loss, yes, she lost several members of her family in a short time. To begin with, her brother-in-law Maximilian, shot down in Mexico, in fact."

He bursts out laughing. She is appalled.

"That's funny? I don't think so."

"Emperor of Mexico, he, a Habsburg. It's a joke, you know it as well as I. Oh, that could be the subject of my next film. I'll think about it. I haven't yet shot a comedy. Would you like to portray Charlotte, his crazy wife? Or Concepción, his Mexican mistress, Concha?"

She reflects.

"I'd like to play Catherine in *Wuthering Heights* ..."

"Too romantic for me."

She reflects for a moment.

"Sofia Perovskaïa?"

A smile crosses his face. He's been thinking for a long time of that passionate activist. He stares at Marjorie intensely, then shakes his head. She is not made for that role. She's disappointed.

"And don't forget her son," she says, after a moment of silence. "Rudolf, Sissi's son."

At that point he almost chokes on a slice of sausage. He grabs the bottle of water, and drinks half of it.

"Oh! The depressive heir who ended up killing himself at Mayerling."

"Some people think he was assassinated because of his liberal ideas. I'd tend to believe that. People have maligned him a great deal. They painted him as a seducer, a madman. He was perhaps simply an idealist."

He admits that all kinds of far-fetched hypotheses have been proposed. There is no longer any proof; his father the Emperor had all compromising documents burned. So, as one can imagine, people invent.

"History is not an exact science, Margot."

"Of course not. Fortunately."

"In any case, it's too big for us; we're too small for it. So we must remain humble."

Humble? Ivan Cristu? She in turn bursts out laughing. Humble? He is anything but.

"Is something funny?"

"Humility is not really one of your qualities."

"Come, eat something: you're only nibbling and I don't like that. Only children of rich people who've never experienced hunger turn their nose up at their plate. The avocados are delicious; you're missing something. Native fruit, like tomatoes, potatoes, corn: we owe them to America. You speak of desire, jealousy, love. You know what? Hunger is what drives the world. Our history is that of our hunger. Tomatoes and potatoes saved old Europe from famine. Eat, Malinche. She was certainly not anorexic."

"But she smoked."

She lights a cigarette.

"Tobacco also comes from America."

Before, Marjorie studied that inexact science, history, enrolled in a masters program, interested in the First World War. She was planning to write her thesis on Mayerling. Everything changed when she filmed an advertisement for a chocolate spread, another for a perfume, *Déesse*, and one thing led to another. Some extra work and very small parts, then Lola, then the Duchess of Devonshire on Broadway. The horrible review from that awful Andy Block, now dead, good riddance, in an attack in Paris last June. It serves him right, she'd rejoiced, learning the news. The great critic had passed away, so full of pretence that he'd exploded. She was avenged. Let him burn in hell. No, better yet, let oblivion swallow him up, oblivion where billions of his fellow men languish, failures like him. Fortunately for her, it was through seeing that play that Ivan Cristu selected her to portray Malinche.

She stubs out her cigarette in the ashtray, goes to light another one, changes her mind, and takes a piece of pineapple with her fingers.

It will not be an easy role. The mother of Mexico, the weeping woman, the traitor, the *lengua*.

"Tonight, I watched an episode of your friend the jaguar," Ivan Cristu says. "The alpha male of TV. In Spanish they call him *pantera*."

"My friend?"

She frowns.

"Didn't you act in the series?"

"A cameo role. I was the corpse, the girl found in an

undergrowth. And quite badly banged up. I just hoped people wouldn't recognize me."

"It seems to me there was a little fling with Lukas Balta, the handsome jaguar."

"You read the tabloids?"

"I read everything. I'm interested in everything."

Did he say everything? With his accent, she's not sure. This time, she lights her cigarette.

"I didn't see him for more than ten minutes. We barely spoke to one another."

"What's happening with your love affair with the singer from that band, Nechaev? Is it Max? Or Alex?"

She does not answer.

"They insinuated there was something between him and that Daphné, the singer with the dyed blue hair. Probably another invention of the gossip media. Are you jealous?"

"I don't even know if you're married, if you have children. Ivan Cristu: is that your real name?"

"My private life remains private, Margarita."

"Mine too. And my real name is Marjolaine."

"I know. Marjolaine Brisbois. You were wise to change it to Dubois."

She extends her hand to him, or he to her; it's hard to say.

≈ At that point, followed by Ernesto, a distraught and soaked Quique rushes across the patio and sweeps into the restaurant where his family is gathered.

"She wasn't there," he says, panting. "She wasn't on the plane. She didn't come."

On the verge of tears, he is spluttering, stammering.

"Didn't come? What do you mean? Did you get the time wrong? The day? Did you phone her? Did she explain?"

Everyone is talking at once. No, he did not get the day or the time wrong. He did not phone. He forgot his cell. His mother Matilda retrieves it from the counter.

"Call her."

Trembling, he dials the number. Someone answers. He speaks half in Spanish, half in French.

She missed her airplane, he explains, after hanging up. An accident on the highway. She found another flight. She'll arrive the day after tomorrow.

The day after tomorrow? Matilda is shattered.

"The sancocho? The shrimp in coconut milk? The cake? It will all spoil."

But Rafa says no, out of the question. Food is not to be wasted.

"We'll eat the sancocho. Come on, kids, take down those balloons for me, break that piñata. Have fun."

Sitting quietly, a bit gloomy, the children now rush forward with cries of joy.

Then, turning to Maria Flor and Concha: "And you, girls, please bring a glass of sangria to the two gringos on the patio. And tell them they're invited to the wedding without the bride."

11

The *End of the World*, Teatime

They take it at four o'clock every afternoon
—it is served to them with cucumber
sandwiches, a strange idea.

Rudolf, Maximilian, Pushkin: all betrayed.

And don't forget her son, Rudolf.

HOPE MARY HAS felt depressed for some time, since that fatal day in March, in fact, a tea that turned out disastrously. That turned sour.

She has, for about thirty years, been writing novels for the *True Emotions* collection. Lucrative work: published in several tens of thousands of copies, the book sold in approximately fifty countries, as far as Russia. But now, after fifty stories or nearly—she's stopped counting—churned out over the years with her brother Philip, inspiration has waned, not to say run out. With her brother, but signed only by her, Hope (she dropped the Mary) Spencer. One or two, even three a year in the beginning, the good years. With action-packed plots—in the end rather similar, it must be admitted—set in Imperial Russia, Japan, China's Forbidden City, Provence, or on the Italian Riviera, only romantic places—Baghdad in the time of the Thousand and One Nights. And always with a happy ending. All that without ever leaving their native city of Torquay, in Devonshire.

It must be said that, with the latest titles, things didn't go very well. They felt, how to say, as if they'd come full circle, especially Philip. What else could they come up with? How to be surprised after all those books? New blood could only be beneficial to their creative process. It was his idea. Hope Mary hesitated; she was certainly right, but he'd insisted. He even laid down an ultimatum: either she agreed, or he'd stop collaborating. Without him, how would she manage? A history buff, he did all the research. So she gave in. To help them, they hired ghost writers or surrogate authors, as they were sometimes called. Lucie, impertinent and arrogant: Philip described her rather as in turmoil, a Ugandan in her twenties, and William, a timid thirty-eight-year-old florist seeking the love he'd never found. The poor man was full of good-will, but the problem was his lousy writing. And to think they were supposed to be there to help them. In the end, it was even more work when the time came to revise.

In the spring, they had their weekly meeting: she, her brother and their two ghostwriters. They had to decide on the next novel Hope would write. William had chosen the Duchess of Devonshire; Lucie would write about the love affair of a conquistador and a young Indigenous woman, Mayan or Aztec, Hope no longer remembers. She'd made a few comments. After all, it was her duty and her right: the novel would appear in her name. And then that stuck-up thing had lost her temper and Philip sided with her, defending her with unusual vehemence. It was the first time he contradicted his sister in public, even in private; he seldom dared to get involved. In one terrible moment, Hope wondered if he hadn't fallen in love with the young madam.

After the event—scene would be more accurate—he departed with Lucie in the rain, ditching her there, humiliated, amid the scones and cucumber sandwiches, and nothing was like before. Even William had followed them.

Their lovely sibling connection had taken a nasty blow. And Hope completely lost what inspiration she had left. The publishers were growing impatient. Because, at the beginning of the year, like it used to be for Agatha Christie, you could count on a new title by Hope Spencer on bookstore shelves. If, in the wings, her brother assisted her, no one knew. It was she who received the phone calls —mostly emails, now. Philip took care of the historical research, whereas their two—whichever name we give them—collaborators churned out the first draft. But, as Philip said, there's no shame in receiving help: the greatest authors have done so. Alexandre Dumas, for example. The great Shakespeare himself, perhaps. Could he have written all those plays, thirty-two not counting the apocryphal works and other poems, in so few years? He died at age fifty-two, Hope Mary's age since the spring. In any case, we're not even sure he existed.

Lucie ended up abandoning her plans to write a Mexican novel, quite simply inconceivable in the "True Emotions" collection. She had returned to the fold, as it were. Not really repentant, but she'd returned and that was what counted, for Philip at least. He must have had some role in this about-turn: Hope would swear to it. The meetings had broken off. Lucie claimed to be working on a modern story, a romance between medical students, one in geriatrics, the other in pediatrics. At least, that's what she said. Time would tell. As for William, despite reworking his text on the duchess, for Hope it remained unpublishable. The heart—at least Hope Mary's—was no longer in it.

Spring and then summer had passed, miserably: she moping in her garden, and Philip wandering God knows where. Truth be told, God wasn't the only one, she also knew, or suspected. And knowing or suspecting it did not improve her mood.

When a person is melancholy like that, there is nothing like a journey. A change of scenery is called for, to put things back in perspective. A cruise: why not? There was in fact that ship called *End of the World*, a name that could not be more evocative, heading out from Venice in September and making a ten-day tour of the Cyclades.

She mentioned it to Philip one evening when, most unusually, he was there for dinner. But he replied that cruises were not his cup of tea, thank you. Too many people, most of them boring, with whom you had to pretend to get along.

She then decided to invite William, with honourable intentions, of course. They each would have their own cabin, so he wouldn't have any illusions. For her, a suite with a balcony, an inside cabin for him. The idea was to take advantage of the journey—distancing is always beneficial—to undertake the next novel. Or at least find the topic.

It was then, against all expectations, that Philip changed his mind. A cruise in the Greek islands, cradle of civilization, of democracy: come to think of it, yes, in the end it was his cup of tea. He needed a change, he too.

But, he insisted, Lucie should come along, a way to consolidate their reconciliation. Otherwise the poor thing would be hurt, especially as William was invited. How to refuse?

Poor William arrived with two enormous suitcases filled with books that he spent his days consulting and annotating in a lounger on the deck, or else in the ship's library when the sun was at its peak. Philip had declared loud and clear that for him, working was out of the question. He intended to take advantage of this week and a half to rest—as if he needed any—to visit the islands and the ruins. With Lucie. Who, as well, had absolutely no intention of setting down to work. Apparently she'd only brought in her flowered knapsack a half dozen multicolour bikinis, a few far too short dresses, and tight-fitting T-shirts.

Out of solidarity with William who was slaving away on the deck—after all, he was slaving away for her—Hope Mary did not disembark at the ports of call either. She took advantage of those moments of calm to chat with passengers, especially two Canadians, Francophone Quebecers, they insisted on pointing out. She, a bookseller in Montreal, said that yes, her books always sold very well in French—and he, a retired English literature professor, rather nice even though he'd read none of her novels. She gave him one, signed. She'd brought along a few copies, just in case. Had he read it? In any case, he never spoke to her of it. A shocking lack of manners.

William had just met up with her in the ship's bistro at teatime and was summarizing what he'd read to her. As for Philip and Lucie, they were roaming around the islands, taking the tango classes offered to passengers, even playing bingo. Bingo!

So William now summarized what he'd read. He began by proposing Christopher Columbus to her, with his great voyages.

"According to what I read, the explorer had an affair with one Beatriz Enriquez, in Cordoba, before his great voyages. The mother of his biographer Fernando."

Christopher Columbus ... She nodded her head, perplexed. Not much is known about his love life. A good subject. To be explored.

"He never married her," he said. "We wonder why. His first wife was already dead."

"People died young then. Died in childbirth, I imagine?"

"I didn't find the information. But he was free; he could have married Beatriz. Especially as he had a child by her."

"I don't like that aspect at all."

"We can arrange things the way we've done before. They could marry in secret."

It is true that they often played with the truth. In a novel, everything is allowed. The secret marriage was a romantic hypothesis. Especially since no ghost would emerge from the beyond to contradict them. In the end, she still said no. It was too close to Lucie's project. The one that had sparked things off. William protested.

"But Lucie's story takes place in Mexico fifty years later. At least. And Beatriz is Andalusian, perhaps a converted Jew."

"No, William. It still deals with a conquistador, and I don't want that."

The following day he suggested Mayerling. She sighed.

"It's already been done too many times. Everything's been written and rewritten on the subject, both true and false. Especially false, if you want my opinion."

She herself had been inspired by it in the past, but refrained from mentioning it. In her novel, the crown prince —he was called Franz, like his father the Emperor, a name that was admittedly more inspiring than Rudolf —fell madly in love with Mary—Hope had let her keep her name—and refused to reign if he was not permitted to marry her. He was not permitted. The two lovers fled to Argentina where they spent happy days while in Vienna people were led to believe the prince had died in a hunting accident. In any case, it is far from her best title: she herself admits as much.

"It's so romantic," William said. "Even the name: Mayerling."

"Romantic? Do you want to know the truth? That prince was an unrepentant womanizer, a syphilitic seducer who rendered his wife sterile. You're deluding yourself, my friend. And you disappoint me."

"But …"

"The death of a pervert in a hunting lodge? The story is distressing, not to mention sordid, William. I see nothing romantic in it."

"What about his mother, the beautiful Sissi? They insinuate that she had another child, a daughter, outside the bonds of marriage, and that girl …"

"You're obsessed by illegitimacy, apparently."

He blushed. He himself was adopted; he has been searching, unsuccessfully, for his biological mother for years, but Hope Mary doesn't know that.

"Anyway, all that's been rehashed time and again. Her reputation is overrated. Sissi was a depressive and had awful teeth, which explains why she never smiled. And I'm tired of her; everyone is. Find me something else."

He found Pushkin.

"The great Pushkin, perhaps? Killed in a duel, which is in fact more noble, to clear his name and that of his wife Elena, falsely compromised."

"Perhaps," Hope Mary said, reluctantly.

"In a grandiose setting, St. Petersburg at the time of the czars. The balls, the palaces, troikas in the snow."

"Mmmmm ..."

"The opponent was a Frenchman, one Anthès."

"Dantès? Edmond, perhaps? Like the Count of Monte Cristo?" Hope Mary exclaimed, enticed all of a sudden.

"Georges-Charles. He was a baron."

"Georges-Charles, I wonder. We'd have to at the very least change his name. I'm not saying no, William. A poet, a maligned wife, a duel in the snow ... There is certainly the material for a novel. But keep looking."

So he arrived with Maximilian, the unfortunate—and improbable Emperor of Mexico, another Habsburg—there's no end to them—abandoned by everyone, executed over there by order of President Juarez without having committed any crime, like Louis XVI in France and Nicolas II in Russia. For the female character, this time they had the choice between Charlotte, his legitimate wife who became crazy with sorrow—although suspected of having had an affair and even a child with a Belgian soldier named Van der Smissen, which offered a new possibility for the plot—and Concepción, the Emperor's Mexican mistress, about whom we don't know much in the end. Or both. The rivalry between the two women for the love of just one man.

"Yet another illegitimate child. And another book set in Mexico," Hope said. "Mexico and its bloodthirsty ways. Let's leave that to Lucie. I'm looking for heroes, you know it. Not victims. Besides, isn't that emperor thought to be a homosexual?"

"That was insinuated," William said. "But it wasn't proven."

Today is the last day. Hope is sitting at their usual table in front of the assortment of sandwiches, scones, and lemon tarts. William has not yet arrived, which is unlike him. Usually, he is always first. Elementary politeness, my dear Watson, Philip would say. In the eyes of the little florist, it would be discourteous to make a lady wait. He's from the old school, and Hope Mary appreciates his gallantry.

She sips her tea, bitter, then vaguely worried. Could something unfortunate have happened to him? Seasickness? Yet the sea is as calm as a lake today. A bad fall? She imagines him with a broken arm or leg. Or worse yet. With him, anything is possible: he's so clumsy. But she would have been told. Unless no one saw him: he goes unnoticed. Unless he just simply lost all notion of time: he's so absent-minded. Unless his watch stopped.

At the moment when, abandoning scones and tarts, she stands up to go look for him, she sees him enter. Emptyhanded: another novelty. Usually he has the notebook where he jots things down and the book he has read. No, really, today, something is wrong with him.

She sits back down, and he, across from her, sits down heavily. She notices that his eyes are bloodshot.

Has he been crying? He reaches for a tuna sandwich, changes his mind, signals to the waiter, and orders a scotch on the rocks.

Silence.

"Have you read something interesting?" Hope Mary finally asks, to break the ice. "Do you have suggestions for me? Time is short, William. And we haven't yet agreed on a project."

He shakes his head. The waiter places the glass in front of it. He swallows it in one gulp, and orders another. Hope is dumbfounded.

"I didn't shut my eyes all night," he says, his voice rasping. "At breakfast I couldn't swallow a bite. Nor could I at lunch; I've eaten almost nothing: you must have noticed."

Yet it's unusual for him to leave food untouched, it's true. Hope has seen him more than once in the morning stuff himself with sausages, home fries, and scrambled eggs, not to mention croissants and other pastries. Nor does he eat lightly at lunch—amazing that he is so puny with that appetite. She nods her head understandingly. An anxiety attack. The poor man is exhausted. Perhaps she's taken advantage of him. She blames herself a bit. True, she has rejected everything he proposed. Perhaps she's been too demanding. Did not advise him. She could have … But no, she has no reason to blame herself. She treated him to this cruise, which he, with his meagre income as a florist, would never have been able to dream of and if he's slaving away all day, it's in an idyllic setting, under the sun, while in Torquay it's probably raining as usual.

She prevents him from drinking the second glass the way he did the first. She places her hand over it.

"I can't take it anymore," he says, whimpering. "For ten days I've been reading heart-wrenching stories; I haven't even gotten off the ship at the ports of call to see the islands. While the others enjoy themselves, I, I am treated like a flunkey ... like a slave, a ..."

"Not at all, William. I have a lot of respect for you, you know I do. I haven't gone ashore either, and I too was working"—now she is lying, but it's to help him swallow the pill. "Besides, there's not much to see, I assure you. Shops filled with souvenirs, all the same, made in China, cafés where the slightest beer or Coke costs you a fortune. You've avoided all those tourist traps."

"My heart is broken: that's how I feel."

"Calm down, William. Take time off. You're too stressed: relax. Eat something. You love scones: these ones are with figs, your favourite. I'll pour you a cup of tea."

"My heart is b ... broken," he says again.

He's not going to start stammering again, is he? He had, however, on her advice, consulted a specialist in Torquay. That ... she was going to think defect, that handicap seemed to have been eradicated. But it's true he seems anxious today. Inconsolable, even.

"Come, William: count to three, breathe deeply. That's what your speech therapist told you to do: what's his name, again?"

He counts, breathes, then:

"Lu ... lug ...

She suppresses, or rather does not suppress a gesture of impatience.

"No, not Lucie," she shouts. Then a bit more gently: "I'm speaking of your therapist."

"Luna!"

Yes, well, Luna. Those kinds of names, where do they find them, you wonder.

"You never un … understood," he says miserably, without stammering or almost, this time.

Of course she understood, has known it since the first day. Or the second. It was inevitable.

He gives up on the tea, and drinks a sip of whiskey, almost choking.

"Is it really the time for declarations, William? Let's take advantage of our last day, let's relax. The captain has promised us a surprise this evening."

"You don't un … understand."

"But yes."

Inevitable. So predictable. She, a successful author, translated into who knows how many languages, and he, a humble anonymous florist in Torquay. She almost pities him.

She blames herself. How, after having read so much, written, meditated on love, how could she not see it coming, this declaration of love?

The prince and the shepherdess, or vice-versa. In the end, it's always been the same story since the dawn of time. The famous novelist and the little florist? How could she have been so blind? But no, she was not blind. She just thought that for him it was a dream, no doubt impossible, but we all need to dream. Otherwise, why would people read the books she writes? In the end, everyone is looking for love—what else to look for? Sentimentality is immortal: wandering souls are legion. She'd even delighted in the idea of being the unreachable star to be admired at night, but in silence. Now he's ruining everything.

She tries once more to look understanding, if not compassionate. There's no point in hurting him.

"Dear William," she says.

He looks up.

"It's impossible, as you well know."

He nods.

"But I was hoping. I ... I ...

"Shhh. Don't say anything more."

He finally resigns himself to taking a mouthful of his scone, chews laboriously, raises his cup of tea to his lips, places it back in the saucer without drinking.

"Falling in lo ... love ..."

"Well yes, it only happens in novels."

"I ... I knew it the first min ... min ..."

"Minute."

"I saw her."

Her? Now he's confusing his pronouns. The poor man is losing it. He's not accustomed to whiskey, it's obvious. Or else the surge of emotion is disturbing his grammar.

"She's ... so beautiful."

But who is he talking about already? Now Hope is disturbed. People say that love is, or makes you blind. All the same. No one has ever paid her that compliment, even less so in the third person. She takes a sip of tea, now lukewarm, which she hates, too bad—she swallows it anyway. Really this wet blanket will ruin all her pleasure today.

"All those stories of betrayal. The great Push ... k ... Ppp ... Push ..."

"Pushkin!"

"Ma ... Maximilian, Rudolf, all betrayed ... My ... My heart is br ... broken."

He is repeating himself. In addition to stuttering. It's exasperating. Hope Mary lets her mind wander. Deep down, she's anxious to return to Torquay, her garden, her house, and to Kitty, her faithful dog. For loyalty, we can always count on animals, fortunately. She's even anxious to see rain again, rain and its melancholy. All this sunshine is giving her a headache. She's had enough of the ship. The cruise was not, in the end, such a good idea. Too many people, as Philip had said. Impossible to concentrate. Novelists are hermits; they need solitude and silence. Nor was William a good idea. He was deluding himself. And they hadn't even found the topic for the next novel. Not very efficient. All he'd done was come up with worn-out stories. Mayerling. Who still wants to write about that? She has to admit, reluctantly, yes, but she has to admit it: Lucie is perhaps unbearable and pretentious, but she has imagination—something William totally lacks, alas.

"I have n ... no more hope," he says, sighing.

Well, so much the better.

"He st ... stole everything from me."

Hope Mary emerges from her stupor.

"Stole? Someone stole from you? Here, on the ship? Your passport? Your money? Your books? Your notes? Who stole what from you, William?"

"Phi ... Philip. Your brother."

"Philip stole from you? Completely absurd. You're talking nonsense."

"She told me ... admitted it to me last night. She had prom ... promised me we would write it together. But she ch ... chose to write it with Philip."

"But what are you talking about?"

He breathed conscientiously, counted to three, swallowed a sip of whiskey.

"The novel by Lu ... by Lu ... ."

"Lucie?"

"The Mexican novel. She'd ... promised me ..."

Suddenly, Hope Mary understands. Everything becomes clear: Philip's evasive looks, his silences, his mysterious absences for six months. He only returned home —when he did return—late at night. She'd thought of some middle-aged affair—the famous mid-life crisis— short-lived, she hoped. With Lucie, perhaps. She preferred not to imagine their trysts. She'd closed her eyes. He'd get over that lunacy—or Lucie. Like the others.

She is dumbfounded. For it wasn't that, and it was a thousand times worse. Those hours he stole from her, stole from her, yes, William was right to treat him like a thief. Those hours he spent writing with the other one, her rival, whereas to her he declared he was fed up with writing. Writing that vulgar book, with its lewd passages, its descriptions of torture and bloody rituals. Lies and betrayal. And the novels they'd written together—he'd never wanted to sign them. Her world collapses.

"I'd done research for her. Read a do ... zen books on the history of M ... Mexico. I knew everything. Cortés, M ... Ma ... Malinche ...

"Who?"

"Malinche. The interpreter of Co ... Co ..."

"That's enough, William."

That explains why the text on the Duchess of Devonshire was not progressing. He was supposed to work for her and had devoted all his free time to Lucie and her damned novel. They had all betrayed her, all deceived her.

"They finished it in … May," William says. "Your publisher has already … accepted it. It will come out in J … January. For the new year."

She grabs hold of the table. She too is going to collapse.

"My publisher?"

"Then, they're going to write one on Sir Rod … Roderick, your … father," he says, as if to destroy her. "Apparently he recorded his secrets in black … n … notebooks"

She had never heard tell of these notebooks. Her head is spinning.

And now the coup de grâce.

"They are going to get m … married."

He raises his hand to order a third whiskey. Oh, let him get drunk. She couldn't care less. Doesn't give a damn. Then, come to think of it, she too needs a pick-me-up. To forget.

"Order one for me too, William. A double, no, a triple. No ice."

12

Post-Mortem in New York

*I spoke with someone called Block, Henry
or Andy, a drama critic for a New York
magazine, a stout guy, very funny,
outrageous. Unfortunately, he wasn't so lucky ...*

*... the assortment of sandwiches, scones, and
lemon tarts.*

"ALL TASTES WILL be satisfied," she said. "Carnivores, piscivores, vegetarians, vegans. Gluten and gluten-free, lactose and lactose-free, all tastes will be satisfied, all tendencies, allergies, intolerances, respected. Kosher, halal ..."

Myriam interrupted her.

"Kosher."

"Yes, kosher, of course. If you like."

The first woman is Victoria Karr, a food columnist better known as Victor, her father's name, in fact, author of several successful cookbooks, including her famous *Recipes from the End of the World*, five weeks on the *New York Times* bestseller list last year, which she almost published under the pseudonym of Audrey Caruso, that time. Here's why: her paternal great-grandfather was called Vittorio Caruso, yes, Caruso like the opera singer. Travelling from his Sicily up to Genoa and leaving from there on the *Nord-America*, in steerage, he disembarked in Uruguay, where he married. His eldest son, another Vittorio, headed North and once in the US changed his name to Karr. He named his son—Victoria's father—Victor, in honour of the pioneer. So Victoria, the eldest of the siblings, is, in a way, part of the family tradition. And her mother's name is Andrea. At the last minute, she abandoned the pseudonym and chose to sign her father's name, as she does for her reviews. Incognito suits her; she doesn't want to be recognized in the street, even less so in the restaurants she reviews and often—let's not mince words—murders with her vitriolic pen. For the next book, *Eating Late at Night*, she has decided, how to say, to come out of the closet, to add the *i* and *a* to her name. The moment has come to appear openly and she will appear in all her glory at the launch planned at Chez Marcel, a trendy French restaurant, in three months. The work will be on bookstore shelves shortly before Christmas. With her real name on the cover, and her photo on the back. Victoria Karr.

The other one, Myriam, is the mother of Andy N. Block, theatre critic for *Big Apple Scene*, who died in an attack at Harry's Bar in Paris last June. He called her Mimi; he found that Mimi sounded French, and he always had a strong weakness for France, Marcel Proust, all that, not to mention the cuisine—he was so fond of food.

They have been friends since adolescence, almost like sisters.

≈ Let's talk about the premiere and of her work, *Eating Late at Night*. To gather information on nighttime gastronomy, she took a big trip around the world last year.

Because, it's true, while to find food in the daytime people can choose among a wide range of gourmet food shops, markets and supermarkets, delicatessens, starred restaurants, and trendy bistros, what do night workers, ambulance drivers and nurses, doctors on call, police officers, and security guards, firefighters, not to mention sex workers, creatures inspired by the moon, night owls for pleasure and other insomniacs eat? They don't have much to nosh on, admit it. Those who have not prepared their snack must often make do with dried-up slices of pizza, prewrapped sandwiches, too often past their best-before dates. The chefs have gone to bed, the espresso machines are unplugged. Coffee lovers have only insipid filtered coffee, or worse still, that revolting liquid, sometimes pre-sweetened, that spurts out of a dispenser into a Styrofoam cup. Pathetic. To such an extent that she almost had to abandon the plan to publish a book on the subject. At night there is no gastronomy. That is what she'd found in America, including Canada—indigestible poutine tested in a greasy spoon in Montreal, her last stop, last spring.

And yet. The trip had surprises in store for her and she did not return empty-handed: it's these surprises, a few recipes, many anecdotes and photos, that make up *Eating Late at Night*. In Sofia, for example, a creamy nettle soup. A simple margherita pizza but oh-so delectable—the quality of the olive oil—in the colours of the Italian flag, eaten in a Neapolitan trattoria at three in the morning. In St. Petersburg, blinis, oscietra caviar—farmed certainly, excellent nevertheless—and *smetana*, on the patio of a restaurant along a canal—in summer, some are open all night—accompanied by a glass or two of iced vodka, a treat. Another night, blintzes and sour cherry jam served this time with tea from a samovar. How to forget? It was at the famous Literary Café, on Nevsky Prospect, where Pushkin had his last cup of chocolate before the fatal duel with his brother-in-law, the infamous Baron d'Anthès. Some have spoken of lemonade, but Victoria doesn't believe he drank lemonade at dawn in the middle of January. A life-size wax statue of the poet awaited her at the entry, with his pen and inkpot. In the afternoon, she visited the palace transformed into a museum where he died after two days of absolute agony. At the end of her visit, in front of the coffin of Alexander Sergeyevich, she burst out sobbing. And what to say of the pata negra ham—the pigs are fed acorns almost exclusively—served in Andalusian *mesones*, in Seville, especially, during a flamenco show, cut into perfect slices, accompanied with sheep's milk cheese just pungent enough, black olives, and a glass of *vino fino*.

Gastronomy is her whole life. Whereas Myriam … a cougar as they're called nowadays, even though she denies it. Her latest conquest did not bring her luck, alas: that's the least that can be said. Truth be told, Andy's mother still feels guilty. After a dismal evening at the theatre—a deadly boring play—it was March, raining, mother and son went as usual to eat in a restaurant, Chez Marcel, actually. During the meal, Andy confided his latest passion to her: he'd set his heart on a Russian, Iouri, and, against all expectations, the Russian appeared at the end of the evening. For Andy, it was unexpected: he quivered, literally. But Myriam used her charm, batting her eyelashes, casting knowing smiles, and stole him from him. A one-night affair, she says. Well, two or three, no more. Nothing serious. A game. Yet after that episode, Andy, outraged, or hurt, left for Paris. He wanted to write a novel, he said as a pretext, needed solitude, distance. And she, still feeling guilty, lent him one of her credit cards.

After the attack, she went to recover what he'd left behind: a laptop computer, a few notebooks—the Mont-blanc she'd given him was not found. In the end, it was not a novel he was writing, but a play, and she played the bad guy: he'd made her a singer on the decline, and utter-ly evil. He had not forgiven her.

≈ Both women are now in Andy's apartment, in Man-hattan. The occasion is what Myriam calls a post-mortem, an evening where people will pay tribute to the prematurely deceased critic. At first, she'd wanted some-thing simple and understated, just a plate of madeleines and a pot of linden tea to mark the event. Andy would have appreciated that allusion to *In Search of Lost Time*, his favourite book; he'd read and reread it, knew it al-most by heart. When he was feeling impetuous, as he said, he would declaim interminable passages from it, in French, to his listeners who didn't understand a word and who, it must be said, would yawn with boredom. But Victoria said no, out of the question. Linden tea and madeleines is not a way to entertain people. And every-one, or almost, likes to eat. "You send out the invitations, I'll take care of the rest."

≈ She arrived earlier with the victuals, "mezze, antipasti, tapas, zakuskis, cucumber sandwiches, just finger foods," not to mention the scones and tarts: raspberry, lemon "for those with a sweet tooth" in cardboard boxes. To her regret, she had to pass up the *serrano, iberico, prosciutto* and other ham, even though she'd come across Andy more than once as he was buying them in Little Italy. He'd wink at her, saying, "*Per favore,* please, not a word to Mimi."

Myriam brought the flowers, cattleyas, another memory of Proust, and champagne. Andy's bar was still well stocked with bourbon, vodka, cognac, and Armagnac.

To tell the truth, this wasn't how she'd imagined the evening. At the start, she just wanted to invite a few friends, sip some herbal tea, dunking madeleines into it, like in the novel, and serve delicate finger foods, since Victoria insisted, while remembering happy, moving times, even comical ones, why not? Her mourning is not over. But no alcohol. Yet, there again, Victoria intervened. "Herbal tea does not encourage confidences," she said. "Your guests will fall asleep and that's not what you want. To open them up you need something stronger. Nothing like it to loosen tongues."

Myriam let herself be persuaded, but in the end, does she want confidences that badly? She herself asks herself that now. Just how far does she want to loosen tongues?

"Believe me, Myriam, you should not only invite friends," Victoria said. "You need some enemies too. That's the only way you'll get the truth."

Friends: did Andy really have any? Enemies, yes, with his profession, certainly. She thought of the last play they'd seen together, that fateful evening. *Moriarty and the Duchess of Devonshire.* He'd strongly panned those involved in his review: the author, to start with, Juliette Evanelli, the novelist who'd recently tackled theatre. Andy had been particularly ruthless with her. But Juliette was busy, that evening. The actors. There were three, a play for a rather limited audience, without a lot of action — "verbiage," as he had written. Brian Fuller (Moriarty), John Wallace (Holmes), Marjorie Dubois (the Duchess), and he had been hard on them as well. Fuller wasn't available; he was acting in a play. Marjorie couldn't be found; she lived in Canada, on the west coast. Currently she was thought to be in Mexico. Only John Wallace accepted. As for friends, Myriam checked Andy's address book and called a dozen of them. All made their excuses: family or business get-togethers, concerts, birthdays. Only one said yes, but he telephoned two days later to cancel. A terrible flu: he didn't want to contaminate them. Short of ideas, she ended up inviting Bruno, a waiter at Chez Marcel, Andy's favourite restaurant. There had been a kind of bond between them. And then, in desperation, Iouri.

≈ "We won't be very many," Myriam says now. "Most declined the invitation."

"How many?"

"Eight, including us."

"So much the better. It will be more intimate."

Moon Oriol, a reviser at *Big Apple Scene*, the magazine to which Andy collaborated, and Leo LeGrand, film critic for the same magazine, arrive together at seven o'clock on the dot; they seem rather stilted, and are the first. Moon clasps Myriam in her arms.

"All my sympathy," she says.

She appears sincere.

"My condolences," Leo says, who seems less so.

Victoria offers them a drink.

"If you prefer, we can make tea," Myriam says.

They both take whiskey. Bruno shows up at seven twenty.

"A good guy," Leo says.

"And what a pen," Moon says. "What culture, what vocabulary. Never the slightest mistake in his texts. For a reviser, it was almost frustrating. Spelling, grammar, punctuation: he mastered everything. I never even had to add a comma."

Leo agrees without, however, too much conviction.

"What an appetite as well," Bruno proclaims in turn. "Incredible what he could wolf down. Right, Mrs. Block?"

She acquiesces with an imperceptible nod. The expression "wolf down" remains stuck in her throat.

"He often had two first courses in addition to the main course," Bruno says enthusiastically. "The entire bread basket, sometimes he even asked for more, butter too, he buttered thickly. It's true that with his build …"

Leo stifles a laugh. Moon gives him a little nudge.

"Two desserts," Bruno says. "Two aperitifs, a bottle of wine for him alone, then liqueurs, two or three. I've seen him, and more than once, leave the restaurant … unsteady, to use a euphemism."

"Fortunately, he wasn't driving."

John Wallace is the fourth. He warns them he can't stay long. He has to see his agent a little later this evening. A crucial meeting, impossible to put off.

"Andy didn't hold back either when we had our editorial committee meetings," Moon says. "One glass after another: scotch, cognac, grappa. It was continuous."

"When he'd had one too many, he'd declaim his monologues to us. Marcel Proust, do you remember?"

"We didn't understand a word."

"He'd say: it doesn't matter. It's for the music of the language, the *imparfait du subjonctif* in French."

Moon bursts out laughing.

"Unbearable. We couldn't wait for him to shut up."

"Or for him to go."

Now they're painting her son as a drunkard. Myriam is offended. Is this a way to speak of the dead, especially when they've met with such a tragic end? No, she broods, that's not how she imagined the evening.

It is five past eight; Franco Liri (no relation to the deceased composer), director of the Mayerling Theatre—off-off-Broadway, has just arrived. Andy had always—almost always—spoken well of their productions, and that was rare. Myriam's hope returns.

Liri places a folder on the table, Andy's unfinished play, that Myriam asked him to evaluate.

"A fair critic," Moon says now, as if to appease.

"A little too severe," Leo says.

Myriam protests: he was demanding, yes, a perfectionist. He was right to condemn mediocrity; too often people settle for it. John Wallace says nothing. Bruno adds his point of view.

"Generous, let me point out," he says. "He tipped generously."

Myriam thanks him with a little nod—even though, usually, it was she who paid the cheque. Bruno wonders what he's doing there.

"With Marjorie Dubois, for example, he went too far," Leo says. "He found favour with only the feather in the hat."

"On that review, he overdid it. He lost control. You wonder what got into him."

"If Dubois had been as hopeless as he wrote, Ivan Cristu wouldn't have chosen her for his next film."

"Cristu himself said it was seeing her in *The Duchess* that triggered something for him."

"In the end, Andy was pretentious."

"A grouch."

"Maybe even jealous."

"Critics often are ... Not you, Leo, of course."

Victoria grabs a plate of canapés and hastens to pass them around.

"Smoked trout," she says, "gravlax imported from Norway, baba ghanouj ..."

Everyone takes one, except for John Wallace, who checks his watch. Sorry, he has to go.

"Andy wrote a play in Paris," Myriam says once she has closed the door behind him. "And I asked Franco to read it."

She indicates the folder on the table.

"The ending is missing; he must have had it in his head, who knows what he was thinking when ... at the last moment. And, I don't know, there are perhaps a few passages, a few lines to rework: it wasn't the final version. We can certainly find a young author to ... Right, Franco?"

Franco does not answer. Presently, all the guests seem a bit ill at ease. Victoria goes to fetch another bottle of champagne from the fridge, offers her tarts.

"Your opinion, Franco?" Myriam says, insisting.

He selects a raspberry tart. He finishes chewing, wipes his lips before deciding to speak.

"Too many flaws, improbabilities. The mother who

seduces the son's sweetie is a bit far-fetched: it's not be-
lievable."

"Oh ..."

"A rehash. You can't get more melodramatic ... The
cake doesn't rise, if you'll allow me a culinary metaphor.
Impossible to rework this play. Unbearable. Inedible.
Unperformable. Sorry, Myriam."

She does not reply. Franco hammers on, merciless.

"Even the title, *Sleepless Nights in Gehenna* ... It's
so pretentious, if not pompous. I scarcely dare to think
what he himself would have said of the play. He would
have destroyed it viciously, believe me."

A long silence follows.

"Well," Bruno says.

He clears his throat.

"All good things come to an end, huh?"

≈ And when Iouri rings the bell, at midnight, they've all
gone. Only Myriam, Victoria and the bottle of champagne, uncorked, remain.

13

The *End of the World*, After Dinner

His granddaughter Vittoria, Vickie, present
right here, on the ship, with her henchman,
a tattooed and rather hefty Argentine,
inherited the rights to Broken Wings ...

"The captain has promised us a surprise
this evening."

... marinated octopus ...

MARJOLAINE HAS JUST finished her dessert, a fig ice cream parfait flavoured with grappa—delicious. Ten days of gourmet dishes, things with white truffles, fish and sea-food unknown in our climate—marinated octopus was even served once, as a first course. According to Béatrice, octopus is now very trendy in Montreal: it's served in all the fashionable restaurants. Perhaps, but Marjolaine did not care for it. To tell the truth, she's looking forward to rediscovering old favourites: her shepherd's pie, for example. Of course, they wouldn't serve you that type of comfort food on a cruise ship. This evening she drank Chablis, a bottle shared with John Paradis: two glasses for her, the rest for him. Béatrice preferred red wine with her rosemary-braised lamb shank. Bordeaux something. Marleau?

"I'd like to go a bit crazy," she said. "But really, the Château Margaux is exorbitant."

Alcohol is not included in the package.

Coffee and liqueurs are going to be served.

"Oh, John, before I forget," Béatrice says. "I found the title of your novel on hell and paradise, *In the Cauldron of the Borgias*."

"Poularde with arsenic? Belladonna carp? Amanita stew?"

She answers yes, that kind of stuff. Then, addressing Marjolaine, she says that the Borgias were supposed to have ..."

"I know. I watched the TV series."

Marjolaine has had more than enough of their condescension. They really take her for an illiterate. It's downright humiliating. She can't wait for Montreal, with Marcel, Denise, Laure and the others.

"Sorry, Marjolaine."

They're always sorry: that's annoying too.

The musicians — they are three: violin, piano and guitar — have been playing soft music, well-known tunes throughout the meal. The captain now approaches the microphone on the stage. After the usual patter, thank-yous and compliments, he clears his throat.

"The surprise," John Paradis says, whispering. "A promise is a promise."

"Although she's travelling incognito, some of you have no doubt recognized our distinguished passenger," the captain says, "a singer from France whose successes are known around the planet."

Heads in the audience look up.

"And even though she's now resting between two

concert tours—before boarding the ship, she played in the Far East, where she met with stunning success; next week she'll be on tour in the Balkans with the Canadian group Nechaev—I asked her a huge favour: to sing her favourite song for us, which is also my favourite, to mark the last evening of the cruise. She graciously accepted. Ladies and gentlemen … Daphné."

He began in French, in homage to the singer. Now he repeats his spiel in English, then in Italian. Delighted murmuring in the dining room when the girl with the sky-blue hair stands and heads to the microphone. She whispers that, to please the captain, she'll sing *Broken Wings*, in memory of Ernesto Liri "who recently left us," she says, looking as afflicted as if she'd been a close friend.

The captain embraces her, kisses her on each cheek and then returns to his seat. The chess players exchange a knowing look. A tall young man in black, with a pony-tail, three-day beard, and dark glasses then steps onto the stage, holding his saxophone. After glancing at one other, the musicians begin, first on the piano, then the violin and guitar. Daphné's voice rises, a reed that swells gradually and transforms into a brook, then a torrent, a river. It's said she studied classical voice, was considering opera before changing paths.

Bird in the rain, watch it fly …

That young bird with broken wings … John Paradis suddenly has an image, remembers a young girl met in the Dominican Republic in the spring. A bird in the rain—even if it was always sunny over there. Concha, Conchitita. Long black hair, minidress in faded colours, toenails with chipped polish. Both cynical and naïve, strong and fragile, resourceful, sad, and funny. He spent a most pleasant week in her company. She claimed to be a sightseeing guide—there wasn't much to see. Together morning, noon, and night. She introduced him to her Uncle Rafa, her Aunt Matilda, her child, two years old, her mother, sisters, and cousins. She even taught him to dance salsa. And she was very indulgent when it came to … let's say his missteps. A lovely week, really. Except that at the end, she seemed to want to mix pleasure and feelings and, for him, that's the worst combination. He's already lived enough to know. His dear Byron would have concurred. He taught the poet's *Don Juan* at university, but the young generation isn't that interested in it. They could learn a lot from him. When, eyes filled with hope, Concha confided to him that her cousin Quique was going to marry a Canadian, he understood what she hoped for from him. Before leaving, he gave her a silver bracelet with a turquoise stone. She asked him, quavering, if he would return. He replied that yes, one day, certainly. What else could he say to her? And yet, this evening, he's a bit ashamed. He imagines her limping in the night, like the pitiful Lola in the movie.

At the first notes, a ripple of applause ran through the audience. Now the saxophone takes up the melody. John Paradis leans over and whispers in Marjolaine's ear.

"Ernesto Liri is the composer. *Broken Wings*, you know, the 1940s movie. He died in Italy early this summer."

"My God!" Marjolaine whispers. "I didn't know that he died."

Because she knows the song, of course, like everyone. People often know songs without knowing who wrote them. She must have seen the movie two or three times over the years. It was even on TV the evening when Doris had her aneurism. An old movie in black and white.

Scenes come back to her: it's almost as if she were still in her restaurant last December 21. On the television screen, a young woman in tears, Lola, that music — someone had turned up the volume — violins accompanying her as she limped in the rain. The villain, a fat bald guy with his cigar, and her handsome lover, who was struck by a bullet in the chest and collapsed in slow motion on the sidewalk. Outside it was snowing. At the End of the World, the others were playing cards. Diderot Toussaint, Laure, Denise, Raoul Potvin. The bathroom door was locked; they'd broken it down, and there was Doris, huddled up between the sink and the toilet, her skirt hitched up, her tube of lipstick beside her.

She closes her eyes. This morning, the discovery of Fanny Laframboise's body, then the traumatic memory hitting her. Life is so fragile. Suddenly she regrets taking this cruise, feels as if she's abandoned those dear to her, afraid of never seeing them again. Life is so fragile. What if the ship sank or their airplane crashed into the sea?

"Are you okay?" Béatrice asks.

Marjolaine nods her head.

"Yes, yes, all is well. It's just that this music ..."

"It brings back memories for me as well."

We'll never know which ones, because a harsh cry has just broken the spell.

Like most of the diners, Marjolaine turns her neck to see what is happening. The pregnant redhead overturned her chair as she stood up; she now advances, staggering, toward the stage, her stomach prominent. She's exchanged her yellow dress for another of the same model, lime green this time, and her pink ballet shoes for what must be twelve-centimetre stiletto heels. Marjolaine is afraid she'll stumble, collapse face down on the floor, maiming her child or children at the same time.

"What is she saying?"

"She wants to know how much Daphné is being paid to sing," John Paradis says, translating.

"Why does she want to know that? It's none of her business."

"Marjolaine is right," Béatrice says. "It's not her affair. Besides, if you ask me she's not being paid. The captain said so: she's doing us a favour."

"Wait ... she's claiming to be Ernesto Liri's granddaughter ... she's called Vickie ... I didn't catch that ... if I understand correctly, she's inherited the copyright to the song; it cannot be sung without her permission ... She says that he never loved her."

"Who's that?" the two women ask in unison.

"She said 'he.' That must be her grandfather, I imagine. Her grandfather didn't love her."

"She's had too much to drink," Marjolaine says. "What does her grandfather's love have to do with all this?"

John Paradis shrugs his shoulders.

"I don't know any more than you, Marjolaine."

"If he didn't love her, he certainly wouldn't have left her the rights to the song," Béatrice says. "If it's true. They must be worth a fortune."

"Yes. She says ... it's confusing. Sorry, I can't follow —they're all talking at the same time."

The captain now strides over to the redhead. He tries to calm her down, but she doesn't calm down. On the contrary, she's still shouting who knows what; her tattooed companion advances in turn, stands between her and the captain. Waiters run over from various points in the dining room. The redhead gesticulates; her companion grabs her arm. She struggles. A glass on the table next to them is broken; red wine spreads across the white tablecloth. It looks like blood. Now he leads her, or drags her, still screaming, outside the ship's restaurant.

The musicians—except for one—have stopped playing; Daphné, alarmed, sings a few words: *Watch it fall ... Broken wings*, then she too falls silent. All that can be heard is the moan of the saxophone in the new-found silence.

14

Opening Night at the End of the World

The opening was planned for September 21,
Charlou Dupont's birthday. This evening, in fact.

... he imagines her limping in the night,
like the pitiful Lola in the movie.

AT THE END of the World, everything has changed. The regulars, if they ever come back, will no longer recognize anything. Only the name remains. Yes, everything has changed. Constance-Louise—Louison to her friends, the patron's girlfriend since last spring, the reason he is now in divorce proceedings—has seen to it, and when Louison has decided something you do not resist. The place has been closed all summer for renovations. The scratched tables, the television that hummed day and night in its corner, the tunes from another century—the twentieth —on the radio, that's all over. Finished, like Capri in the old song. Gone too are the shepherd's pies, poor man's puddings and poutines, au gratin or not. At the same time as Marjolaine, the chef with no imagination. It was long overdue.

That—Marjolaine's departure—was not done light-heartedly. At least the owner, Jean-Charles Dupont, was not lighthearted when it came to delivering the sentence. Fifteen years of loyal service, a waitress before becoming a cook—I don't know if you realize, Louison. Impossible to find a more dedicated employee. Reliable, never sick: she barely took a day off. And the customers adored her. How do I tell her she's being let go? Well, yes, Louison realized. Precisely. And, if he did not inform Marjolaine, she'd be the one to do so, and it would no doubt be less courteous. They'd already waited too long. Without a radical change—the customers too had to change—without a concept, as she said, they were headed straight to bankruptcy.

A slunch or cocktail buffet, always trendy, is the concept Louison prefers. The restaurant will be open from five o'clock during the week and at four o'clock on weekends. And, if things go as she hopes, they could contemplate the possibility of a Sunday brunch. And why not a tea dance once a month? Apparently in Paris they're back in fashion. People in their fifties, and even young people, would love it. Waltzes, tangos, boogie-woogies: participants would wear vintage clothing. But they mustn't rush anything: they have to begin by building customer loyalty. Building loyalty is key. The new chef, Guillaume, fresh from the Institut d'hôtellerie, has come up with extraordinary recipes, some made with octopus or kangaroo. He only uses organic, fair trade products, and free range eggs that he himself picks up at the farm: the trendy people in the neighbourhood will love it. The kitchen has been expanded; it is now open and customers will see him perform. He boasts that he is an artist and refuses to carry out his art in a cubbyhole.

On each table, a slender vase in frosted glass, and in each vase, a rose just starting to bloom, white, red, pink, yellow. And even a blue one, unusual, unique and very expensive—after all it's the opening night, no expense will be spared—in bloom, in full view on the counter they now call the bar. Behind the bar, a large mirror in which a variety of bottles set on glass shelves is reflected.

In the back room, where middle-aged women and taxi drivers used to gather for their Wednesday night card games, the back wall is a vivid turquoise, calling to mind an exotic sea. Posters of tropical or fiscal paradises—Bonaire, Paradise Island, with their moonlight and palm trees adorn the other walls. An upright piano is now on display in a corner. This evening, Vanessa will play, on other evenings too, and on weekends. She's the owner's daughter, the youngest of his three children; she has studied piano since the age of six and has just been admitted to the conservatory. His son Pierrick will help out in the kitchen, assisting Gabriela. As for Kim, the eldest daughter, she is now touring around the Aegean Sea, having found work as a chambermaid on a cruise ship. Going by what she writes in the email sent yesterday, she's not about to return. "With the tips, I'm making quite a bit of money," she wrote. "And you know what? My ship is called the *End of the World*. And our Marjolaine is on it." Louison doesn't understand how the former cook was able to afford such a trip. Did she receive an inheritance? Win a million in a lottery? Jean-Charles chose not to tell her about the severance pay. Let Marjolaine enjoy it like that: so much the better. He is happy for her.

Vanessa came up with this idea: a giant screen featuring excerpts from cult films while she improvised based on the musical soundtracks: *India Song*, *The Godfather*, *The Umbrellas of Cherbourg*, *Once Upon a Time in the West*, *Broken Wings*, *A Man and a Woman*, *Casablanca*.

For today, she chose those. Seven. Customers may propose others and place their suggestions in a box on the piano. Louison thinks it is an excellent way to ensure their loyalty.

Five after seven, the guests, friends and family, clients of Constance-Louise—she's a real estate agent—and shopkeepers in the neighbourhood begin to arrive. For her inaugural cocktail buffet, Louison, wearing this evening for the first time a sand-coloured designer outfit over a coral silk camisole, designer as well, invited people for seven o'clock—that's what the invitation said, sent by mail and not over social media, which, for her, totally lacks elegance. On the envelopes, Vanessa and Pierrick had handwritten the addresses.

Handshakes, embraces, kisses on both cheeks. Friends and relatives wish Jean-Charles Dupont happy birthday; some have even brought a present. Scents of perfume waft and mingle in the room. Everyone goes into raptures. The admiring oohs and ahs, whether or not sincere, come from all sides. The borough mayor, the city councillors, and two MPs are supposed to make an appearance later in the evening. Guillaume's elegant hors d'oeuvres are artistically displayed on trays; in their buckets, bottles of sparkling wine wait to be uncorked. A patio has been set up on the sidewalk; it is still twenty-eight degrees—unusual to see such heat in Montreal in late September.

A close-up of Lola appears on the giant screen, and it's the famous scene where, having broken the heel of her shoe, she totters in the night. Then the apotheosis: her lipstick in hand, she writes these words on her bedroom mirror: Forgive me. Some folks hum the words to the song while Vanessa plays the melody on the piano.

That is when Raoul Potvin bursts in, spoiling the scene, looking slovenly amid the guests in their finery.

"I want the holiday special," he blurts. "Turkey and the works!"

He advances uncertainly, jostling people, chairs, tables. A vase and its white flower find themselves on the floor. Gabriela rushes up with a broom and dustpan.

"Get this nutcase out of here," Louison says. "He's completely drunk."

"I'm not drunk!" he shouts. "I want turkey with cranberry sauce, and tourtière, and sugar pie!"

He's not completely smashed; he only drank four beer before leaving home. Or five, he didn't count. No matter: he's not drunk. Not yet. Just frustrated. Furious.

"Where's Marjolaine?"

As if he didn't know she no longer works at the End of the World. Everything is known, news spreads in the neighbourhood at the speed of light. Jean-Charles Dupont takes his arm, tries to lead him to the exit.

"Come on, Raoul, be reasonable. This evening, you see, we've organized a small celebration among friends. Come back another day. Tomorrow, if you like. You'll always be welcome."

But he resists. Raoul Potvin doesn't feel like being reasonable.

"There's always been a holiday special at the End of the World," he yells. "Or there was the sugar shack special: beans and maple syrup dumplings."

Louison is on the verge of calling the police. Dupont

motions to her to not worry; he's controlling the situation. A few guests whisper; others suppress laughter. The holiday special in this heatwave, what a strange idea. Constance-Louise is mortified.

"Gabriela," Jean-Charles Dupont says, "bring some coffee for our friend Raoul. A strong espresso. A double. And a plate of canapés: I'm sure he's famished."

He manages to usher him out, has him sit down at a table on the patio. A slightly shocked Gabriela places a cup of coffee in front of him. Not knowing what he'd feel like eating, she prepared a sweet plate for him: a deconstructed lemon tart, a Chinese pear upside-down cake, also deconstructed. And, as he mentioned cranberries, she added the cranberry soup with grey pepper. The tart and soup in their glass jars, the upside-down cake in a tiny pagoda-shaped ramekin.

"These are Chinese pears," she says, stammering.

He doesn't answer her. Then: "With Marjolaine, we always had marble cake. And she served it with two scoops of ice cream. And we had big cups for coffee."

Gabriela tiptoes away.

"Why did you change everything, Dupont? Now we have nowhere to go. We liked it the way it was, the End of the World. We felt at home. We were happy here."

He says that even though he's not set foot there since the evening of the fateful incident, when he burned Diderot Toussaint's winning lottery ticket. He didn't dare show his face again. Even if he was within his rights do so: Toussaint and he went partners on lottery tickets. The wins were supposed to be divided fifty-fifty. But that hypocrite bought one for him alone, behind his back, won, and refused to share. The others have still not forgiven him, he knows. He also knows that they'll play cards this evening, at Denise's, and that he won't be there.

He takes a bite of the tart, pushes the glass jar away.

"Marjolaine's lemon meringue pie was better than this thing."

Then he stands up and moves away heavily without touching the coffee.

≈ At the wheel of his taxi, Raoul Potvin goes up Saint-Denis. He's driving without a license: it was suspended when he ran a red light under the influence. He doesn't give a damn. He drives cautiously, doesn't want to be stopped, asked for his papers, have to blow into a balloon. Out of the question to wind up in prison. Besides, he didn't hurt anyone that time, and it's not true the light was red: it was still amber. Raoul remembers perfectly; he hasn't yet lost his memory. But the breathalyser spoke, and contradicting it was out of the question.

He now moves onto Boulevard Métropolitain, toward the Laurentian autoroute.

His problem is he can't manage to control himself. His wife often criticized him for it. She'd say: "You have a short fuse, Raoul. You have to learn to moderate your outbursts. Master your instincts, Raoul. You're too quick-tempered." Now that she's gone, there's no one left to calm him down when the anger rises inside him. And it's true that he drank less when she was alive. He drank less. He wonders if he shouldn't sign up for Alcoholics Anonymous. Perhaps he'd make new friends in a group of reformed drinkers like himself. He'd begin to play five hundred again, or dominos, or checkers—anything to pass the time.

He hardly sees his children anymore. When Jessica invited him for supper the last time — it was for Father's Day — he got angry. She hadn't made the shepherd's pie the way her mother made it. For him, that was a sacrilege, no more no less. She'd replaced the minced meat with lentils. A vegetarian shepherd's pie. He didn't finish his plate. He shouted: "And what are you going to serve me next time? Tofu?" He left, slamming the door. He shouldn't have. Shouldn't have gulped down a six-pack of beer before going there. Since then, no news.

"Okay, Francine, I've decided, I'll call her, I'll apologize. Then I'll go to AA. I'll take control, I promise. You're right. It can't go on like this. My life makes no sense anymore, Francine. No sense. I have no more friends. Did I ever have any? A friend, a real one, is capable of forgiving, even when it's hard. Those guys, they won't forgive me. No, I hadn't any friends, I realize that now. Just partners at cards and in the lottery. I had only you."

He is speaking to her out loud; he's sure she's there, somewhere, and from where she is, she's listening to him the way she always did. In any case, he hears her voice.

"No sense," he says again. "I'm going round in circles like a bear in a cage."

He remembers that she called him "my teddy bear" in their private moments. He feels like crying.

"And there's something that I never wanted to tell you; I never wanted to hurt you. The last months of your illness, Marjolaine and I ... It happened two or three times, no more, I swear. But I want you to know there was never any love between us. It's just that you were so sick, you had no more strength and I had needs. You were no longer able to satisfy them. I wasn't mad at you.

I needed consolation, mostly. Aside from Marjolaine, I was always faithful to you; I swear. You're the only one I loved. I don't know what she felt; we never talked about it. Perhaps she took me out of pity."

Now he's on the 15, the Laurentian Autoroute. Night has fallen. He heads north, has no idea where he wants to go. To Saint-Faustin, perhaps, or Sainte-Agathe-des-Monts, or farther. Mont-Laurier. Then he'll stop in a motel to spend the night. He'll return to Montreal tomorrow morning, clean the house, throw out all the beer bottles awaiting him in the fridge, the rye and the brandy as well. Then he'll sign up for Alcoholics Anonymous, and find a sponsor, someone to call when the desire to drink becomes too urgent.

"Nothing's going right since you left, Francine. Sometimes, I feel as if I'm drowning, and you're no longer there to pull me out of the water. There's no one to throw me a lifeline. I just want to join you where you are. But you're surely in heaven, you were an angel, you believed in it, those things, but I ... Anyway, if it does exist, your heaven, with the life I'm leading — they won't let me in."

He turns on the radio. The news is on: Minister Masson has resigned; the body of the Laframboise girl has been found in Georgia. A new murder has been committed in Montreal on Boulevard Pie-IX. As usual, nothing to enliven the evening. He prefers silence.

In Sainte-Adèle, he notices the sign indicating Sainte-Marguerite-du-Lac-Masson. Oh, like the Minister who resigned. That gives him an idea. There are picnic tables by the lake. He'll sit down there, reflect a bit as he watches the moon tremble in the water. Nothing is more beautiful. He continues slowly along the road; the way is poorly lit. Reaching Sainte-Marguerite, he turns onto Rue des Pins. The condos along the river have burned down recently; he wants to see the scene of the fire.

Nothing is left, or almost. A few walls spared by the fire still stand like ghosts amid the rubble. Potvin parks in front of the deserted street, turns off the engine and exits the car.

"It looks like my life, this scene, don't you think, Francine? It will change, I swear it, my life. I can rebuild it. You'll say that I already promised you that, that I didn't keep my promise. But I'll keep it this time, I swear. You're never too old to stop doing crazy things. One day at a time, like they say in AA, one day at a time, and in the end, you've made amends. You're new; it's as if you were born a second time."

They've built new condos around the marina. Deluxe, this time, with a heated pool, gourmet restaurant, gym, massage rooms, a front desk open day and night. Of course they're more profitable for the city. Perhaps that explains the fire, who knows? Raoul wonders. The cat will be let out of the bag in the end, the truth will be exposed. Or else we'll never know. There has been arson already in the Laurentians, more often than you might think, going by what he's heard. And not only in the Laurentians. It's the same everywhere. Money laundering, insurance fraud and other underhanded practices. Everyone trying to swindle others. The world is corrupt.

He remains there, listening to the river. It continues to flow as if nothing is wrong, joyously, even, it's as if it is singing. There is no one to annoy it; perhaps it is content.

It is still so warm you'd think you were in the middle of summer. To think of it, he doesn't need a motel. Why waste the little money he has? He'll go to the marina, sit down at a table, throw pebbles in the water. As a child, he always won stone skipping contests: a real champion. He can smoke cigarettes while waiting for the day to break. There's a restaurant there, surely too expensive for him. But he saw a snack bar on the road. He hasn't eaten all day.

"Tomorrow morning, I'm going to have a good breakfast, Francine, like the ones you made me when you were here. Eggs, bacon, sausages, toast, coffee. Sometimes, there were even pancakes with syrup. You were always in the kitchen when I came back from my nights in the taxi or when I'd played five hundred until the wee hours with Denise, Boris, and the others. You were so nice. You forced me to drink orange juice for the vitamins. I'll order a big glass tomorrow morning."

He wants a cigarette, feels his shirt pocket. His pack is back in the taxi.

"While waiting for them to give me back my license, I'm going to stop driving. I'll put up posters in the neighbourhood, offer my services as a painter, do little renovation jobs in houses. You know how I was always good at doing odd jobs around the house. I was always the one who repaired things that were broken. And I'm going to learn to cook. My life makes no sense anymore. I'm not eating right; it doesn't help me. Just frozen stuff that I heat up in the microwave. Especially since I'm no longer going to the End of the World. The other restaurants in the neighbourhood have gotten too fancy. How do they say it? The neighbourhood has become gentrified, something like that. And even the End of the World, now. I went earlier; they gave me who knows what in little glasses, called it cranberries—stuff that was impossible to eat."

A figure emerges suddenly from the ruins.

"Hey, big guy, you talking to yourself?"

Raoul Potvin gives a start. He thought he was alone, it's true.

"Good lord, you scared me. You're nuts! Where did you come from?"

"Where did I come from? Well, you see where I'm coming from. I'm coming from hell."

Raoul has heard that, when there's a fire, vandals steal everything that can still be of use, stainless steel sinks, thermostats, door handles, faucets. It must be one of those vultures. Or else he's homeless, squatting wherever he can.

The stranger approaches: now he's very close. Despite the streetlamps lit on the other side of the street, everything on this side is in darkness, and Raoul can't make out his face. The man is wearing a white T-shirt, and holding something in his fist.

"Is that your car?"

"Whose do you think it is?"

"Is there gas in it?"

"Enough to get me to Abitibi. Why, do you want a lift?"

"Stop your stupid jokes, guy. I've just stabbed my girlfriend, so I'm in no mood to listen to your nonsense."

Oh, the domestic drama they were talking about earlier on the radio.

"On Pie-IX, was it?"

The guy opens his hand. He'd been hiding a switch-blade in his fist.

"With this knife."

There's a click: the tip plunges between Raoul Potvin's ribs. Not very deeply, but blood seeps onto his shirt.

"It's not a lift, I want, old man, it's your car."

Because there are two of them and the second one is now at his back. Raoul didn't hear him arrive, but he feels something cold—the barrel of a revolver?—press against the back of his neck.

"Because there's no more gas in mine," says the first one.

With a nod of his head, he indicates a dilapidated car parked at the back of the lot nearby.

"What do we do about it, Francis?" the other one is growing impatient. "We're not going to spend the night here. Should I put a bullet in his head and then we take off?"

"Too much noise. We'll wake the neighbours on the other side of the street. I have a better idea. Wait for me a minute. It won't be long."

Francis enters one of the condos still standing, returns with some electric wire.

"Okay, big boy. Walk."

They have him cross the parking lot, the plank bridge, and enter the little wood that runs along the river. They walk a few hundred metres, stop beside a maple tree.

"Your keys," orders Francis. "And your money, your papers. Hurry."

The other one's revolver is pointed at him. Raoul takes out his wallet from his back pocket.

"The keys are in the car," he stammers.

"That better be true, else we'll come back. And then ..."

207

"You won't have a chance."

"Now, undress," orders Francis.

He kicks him in the shins. Pain radiates throughout his body.

"Faster."

The other one, a tall brown-haired guy, unshaven—Raoul can now make out in the moonlight—sniggers.

Raoul Potvin has never been a coward; he's strong, and has never been the kind to let himself be intimidated. He has always been able to defend himself. But now they're two against him, and they're armed. So he obeys without even trying to discuss the situation. With maniacs like that, no doubt drugged up to their ears, it's the only thing to do. He'd just like them to let him keep his underwear. They don't. Blood seeps slowly from the cut on his chest.

Francis ties him up, hands behind his back, and surrounds his neck with a length of electric wire that he connects to his ankles. The knots are very tight. They tie him, completely naked, to the maple tree, stuff one of his socks in his mouth, wrap his stained shirt around his head, and throw the rest of his clothes in the water. The other one sniggers again. It sounds as if he is braying.

"It's nice out tonight. The big teddy bear won't be cold."

"Speaking of teddy bears, if one comes along, he'll have a feast."

Teddy bear. If that makes them laugh, Raoul stifles a sob beneath his gag.

"And when they find him, we'll be in Abitibi."

They abandon him there, on the ground in fetal

position, powerless, humiliated, shivering in the damp night.

Francine," he calls in his head. "Francine."

But he can no longer hear her voice.

≈ And during that time, at the End of the World, order has been restored. The celebration is in full swing.

15

The *End of the World*, Late Evening

… and that map of the world — dotted with grey areas …

The moon quivering on the sea.

Lies and betrayal.

… blood seeps onto his shirt.

ON THE SHIP, calm has returned. The passengers, at least most of them, now head to the theatre, to watch the final show of the cruise. Philip and Lucie linger on the deck.

"I don't feel like seeing the show," she says. "You?"

He shakes his head.

"I've really had enough of all the fuss," he says. "How about we go to my cabin? I have to change my shirt anyway."

Because it was Philip's glass that was overturned on the tablecloth when the irate girl practically collapsed on him. And his striped shirt now sports a reddish stain near the heart, as if the tip of a knife had grazed him and blood seeped out. She was protesting about something, but what? She was speaking — shouting rather — in her language; they didn't understand a thing she was saying.

"Strange that neither Hope Mary or William came to dinner," Lucie says.

They are now on the cabin balcony. Philip has replaced his stained shirt with a grey and white striped polo shirt. He places a bottle of gin, tonic water and glasses with ice cubes on the table. A bowl of salted nuts as well — it's always wise to eat something when drinking alcohol, even if you're not hungry.

He describes how he went to see his sister, but she wouldn't open the door. Not feeling well, a terrible migraine, apparently. She wasn't hungry, couldn't swallow anything.

Lucie shrugs her shoulders.

"A kind of seasickness? Odd."

"At least that's what she told me through the door, in a small, tearful voice. She took pills, was going to try to sleep. As for William, he can't be found. I wonder where he's hiding. Unless he's fallen into the water."

Lucie is ill at ease. She sighs.

"I think I talked too much, yesterday evening."

"To whom did you talk, my angel?"

"To William, in fact. I told him everything. Your father's notebooks, our novel that will be published, our wedding on the day of the release. I felt euphoric. I'd had a bit too much to drink, I think."

She lights a cigarette. So does he.

He understands: Lucie told William everything, who must in turn have told everything to Hope Mary today, during their tea. The return home will not be easy. Sighs, eloquent silences, reproaches: he anticipates the worst. Red eyes, perhaps even the sound of stifled sobs behind closed doors. She would have ended up finding out, of course, but he'd have rather told her the news himself.

He would have done so gently. Whereas William ... Bitter, no doubt—hardly surprising. Heaven knows how he presented it to her. Not surprising that she has a headache. Lucie says she is sorry.

"Don't worry about it. She'll get over it," Philip says, not really believing it.

She bursts out laughing.

"Yes, come to think of it, she and William will make a good team. The next title for Pure Emotions: *Lies and Betrayal*.

He is not sure he finds that funny.

"I talked too much," Lucie says again, in a hesitant voice. "He ordered champagne, and ..." As if that excused her.

"But I didn't want to," she says. "He manipulated me."

Little William, manipulative? Difficult to imagine.

"I shouldn't have."

"No, you shouldn't have."

Now he's in a real mess. He wonders if it wouldn't be better to move out right away. Living together could become unbearable. Besides, he's had more than enough of living in Torquay with his sister. After the wedding, he'll settle in London, with Lucie. Or, better yet, they could change countries. He invested his money wisely. His income would allow them to enjoy a peaceful existence in Provence, for example, or in Andalusia, a place where the sun shines three hundred days a year, whereas on the shores of the English Channel you can count on both hands the number of nice days. Or on a Greek Island, as others before them have done, such as Leonard Cohen and Lawrence Durrell. This cruise has given him ideas. Life isn't expensive there: he'd buy a white house near the sea, a small boat or a sailboat. In the mornings, he'd go fishing. They'd have a few lemon trees, grow tomatoes in a vegetable garden. They'd only have to learn the basics of the language. But is this the life Lucie dreams of? Of course not. What would she do in a vegetable garden?

≈ It's true, William is nowhere to be found. Probably holed up in his cabin, refusing to answer. But answer to whom? The tragedy of his life is that no one has ever knocked at his door. As for Hope Mary, it's not true she has a migraine. Now she's strolling on the deck, basically deserted at this hour. Almost deserted: a young man has just lit a cigarette, seated at the table where two passengers played chess every morning of the cruise.

The moon is quivering on the sea. That sentence suddenly goes through her mind and she tells herself it is a pretty image. Evocative, yes, romantic: she could use it in her next novel. In the past tense, of course: she always writes in the past tense. The young couple would be leaning against the rail of the yacht — or is it an ocean liner — heading toward ... the place remains to be determined, in any case to a better world. Their blond heads touch. And the moon would be quivering on the sea. Or the black water. Black water is certainly more dramatic. She'll think about it.

No, she won't think about it. Because she won't write anymore, she knows. This business has broken her. She has no more momentum, no more ideas, if ever she had any. It was Philip who had the ideas, and Lucie, recently. William: useless to speak of. He'd rewritten the novel inspired by the tumultuous life of the Duchess of

Devonshire a good half-dozen times without getting any-where. Despite all the advice she had given him. Never going beyond ten words a sentence, for example, else the reader — most often female — would lose interest. Conci-sion, precision, she repeated to him in every possible way. He always went beyond, as if incapable of controlling himself. All those useless adjectives and adverbs.

All that is over. She is tired. She'll retire and live on her royalties. Very comfortably.

She didn't miss a word of the conversation between Philip and Lucie, earlier, when he told her dreadful things about Sir Roderick, their father, spicing up his words with "my heart," "my angel," and "my dear child." Ap-palling, there is no other word. They were speaking free-ly, not suspecting she was on the deck, nearby, within earshot. Of course they thought she was in her cabin with a migraine. But she could make out each word clearly, except when they whispered. She hasn't heard them for a few minutes: they are no longer on the balcony. Not hard to imagine what they're doing now in the cabin. Hope Mary would rather not imagine. That girl is a monster, a man-eater and Philip sees nothing. She began by enticing William, then ensnared Philip. The famous mid-life crisis blinds people.

She thinks again of the conversation she overheard ... So Sir Roderick, in a high ranking position at Scotland Yard, in charge of fraud prevention in the arts, wrote, unknown to everyone, his memoirs in black note-books — five bound notebooks — that Philip discovered in a locked suitcase, black as well, in the attic of the house in Torquay? Unlikely. Had there been a locked suitcase, she would have found it long before he: she knows every corner of the house by heart. Their father involved in the affair of a stolen painting, a genuine or fake Murillo, in the sordid murder of its owner who was kidnapped, starved, and tortured to extract it from him? Philip invented that, for sure; he always had an imagination, more imagination than she, in fact. To make himself interesting in the eyes of stuck-up Lucie; she can see no other explanation. Although ... Their father was, how to say, opaque at times, his profession of course required it. True, in the end, when he was dealing with forgeries and all that, he made many trips to the continent. Rome, Berlin, Madrid, very often Paris. It's true also that when he returned from Paris, he seemed a bit, how to say ... lewd? No, lewd is certainly not the appropriate term to describe their father. In his eye there was a kind of ... perhaps a mischievous gleam? In any case, there was a gleam. But to go from there to imagining him in a liaison with one Margot, a dancer at the Folies-Bergère. Inconceivable. And that Lucie who burst out laughing. Hope nearly shouted at her brother to shut up. She contained herself: she wanted to see how far he'd go in his lies. Although ... She admits she could not suppress a small smile at the thought of Sir Roderick Spencer, such a dignified man, who demanded of his fellow men the same dignity, in Parisian places of debauchery, watching girls raise their legs while lifting their petticoats—did they still dance the French cancan back then? She's no longer sure. In any case, if you believe Philip, the Margot in question was a kind of stripper—their father got an eyeful and worse still. Was it true? You live with people, think you know them, and overlook large sections of their lives. Our story is filled with gaps, grey areas on the map of the world.

It is this story of the stolen painting that they want to explore. Not to write a book. Lucie sees the larger picture: she wants to study script development, go into film. Well, they'd better change their names, else she'll sue them. This time, justice will not be an empty word.

She hears music coming from the ship's discotheque. The show has ended. The young people dance, drink, celebrate. She never danced. She merely described waltzes, polkas, tangos in her novels, a hand around a waist, cheek to cheek. And life passed. She will not dance. She wrote romances while life passed her by, while others danced.

Yet she did have a romance, with Frank, at age nineteen. But Sir Roderick didn't like him. And why didn't he? Because Frankie—which explains perhaps why her male characters are often named Franz, Francisco, Francis, François, Francesco—was a member of the Communist Party. Due to his position as superintendent, Sir Roderick had contacts in every milieu. He vetoed the relationship as soon as he learned of it. "An anarchist? Never! The Spencers are a respectable family." Anarchists, Communists, Bolsheviks: for him, it was one and the same. All revolutionaries, cranks who planted bombs under trains, assassinated the czars and their families. Gallows birds—an expression that made Hope Mary shudder in horror each time she heard it. And Sir Roderick said it often. He was a monarchist, always loyal to his king or his queen. The very idea that someone could make an attempt on the life of a sovereign made him wild with rage, verge on apoplexy. So she, the obedient daughter, obeyed. Perhaps she didn't love Frankie that much, she thinks now.

The sea is calm, tonight: it sings a lullaby. Yes, it sounds as if it is singing. The sea is calm, voluptuous and dark, silky and soft like a bed. You almost want to sink into it. Her characters thought about that sometimes when she or Philip was melancholy. Mary, for example, thought about it when she leaned, motionless, over the waters of the Danube, in the moonlight. Never would the Emperor accept that morganatic union. But at the last moment, when everything seemed desperate, a hand touched her shoulder. Franz. "I reserved our cabin on the *North America*, my love. We are leaving tomorrow. I have abdicated; I will not reign over Austria-Hungary. We'll go live in Argentina." But no helping hand will ever come and touch Hope Mary's shoulder, she knows. Not this evening or ever.

Philip proposed they write a novel on her romantic disappointment, changing the ending, of course. Frankie would tear up his party card, enlist in the army, or they'd flee together to the new Soviet Union, so promising at the time. She'd refused. This romance, her own, her only romance, she wanted to keep for herself, like a daydream.

She didn't go to dinner, didn't want to see anyone, and couldn't care less about the captain's surprise. But she ordered a meal to be brought to her cabin: cream of asparagus, truffle risotto, sole with white butter sauce, Grand Marnier soufflé, Bourgogne Aligoté. She wasn't very well going to let herself die of hunger. She'd done the same thing in her youth, when her pain was, she claimed, too much for her. She would shut herself up in her room while the others ate. When they were in bed, she'd go down to the kitchen, noiselessly, and prepare a plate. She'd always loved food, which is not a failing.

In the end, she could indeed write it, her swan song. She doesn't need them: they have only harmed her. It is Philip who made her believe she had no more ideas, that she was only repeating herself. The truth is that he was speaking of himself when he said the source had run dry. The girl, Irish, would be called Peggy, Molly or Deirdre, yes Deirdre. Or Hope, like herself? Why not? The station platform, then the train taking her to Soviet Russia. Frankie awaited her there.

No, better yet. The time has come to switch gears. Innocent young things and damsels: that time is over. Bashful lovers, unhappy princes: we've seen enough of them. They want blood and tears? They will have them. She has never written about vengeance. The title Lucie mentioned earlier, laughing: *Lies and Betrayal.* We'll see who has the last laugh.

16

Florence, South Carolina, in the Middle of the Night

They found the young Laframboise girl.
At least what remains of her.

Both cynical and naïve, strong and
fragile, resourceful …

ON THE SIDE of the highway, the motel is called, unremarkably, *Sweet Dreams*. It is not much to look at, but for what people go there for, what does it matter? We are in Florence, South Carolina, two hundred and eighty-eight kilometres from Savannah, Georgia, where were found the remains of Fanny Laframboise, the Quebec teenager who disappeared in St. Petersburg, Florida last December. About two and a half hours by car travelling at an average speed of a hundred and ten kilometres an hour.

The man who just entered unit thirty-three never exceeds the speed limit.

His age? Impossible to determine. Mid-thirties, mid-forties, perhaps a bit less, perhaps a bit more. Average height, dark hair, three-day beard, dressed in black jeans and turtleneck, running shoes. He tosses his nylon overnight bag, also black, on the bed. In the room he detects the smell of disinfectant—or insecticide—but regardless, he doesn't intend to stay long. He turns on the bedside lamp, then the TV, removes a bottle of vodka from his nylon bag, pours himself a glass, and settles into the rather ugly and threadbare beige armchair. It is midnight; his program is about to begin. On this channel—they broadcast American series only—it's on at the same time every night.

After the musical theme—harrowing music played on the synthesizer—we hear the voice of Lukas Balta who recites, as he always does—it is a kind of introduction that sets the tone, as it were, of the episode—an excerpt from *The Divine Comedy*.

Midway in our life's journey, I went astray from the straight road and woke to find myself alone in a dark wood.

"Oh!" the man in the motel says. "The straight road. I know it, that quote. *Hell,* Canto 1. Oh, I have another one for you, Sullivan: *Because thou peerest forth Athwart the darkness at too great a distance, It happens that thou errest in thy fancy. Hell,* Canto 31. Not bad, huh? And what do you think of: *And now begin the dolesome notes to grow Audible unto me; now am I come There where much lamentation strikes upon me. Hell,* 5. I always liked that one. What do you say? And my favourite, from Purgatory, this time: *Attend not to the fashion of the torment, Think of what follows.* Think of what follows. There is certainly food for thought. Oh! That Dante Alighieri, what a writer! One never tires of saying it. *The Divine Comedy.* Well, if purgatory is not my favourite, I admit it has its charms, but paradise, what a bore! Personally, hell is what interests me: you understand. The torments that guy invented! If he hadn't been a poet, he'd have been a serial killer, for sure. In any case, know that

I appreciate what you're doing to bring him back to the public eye. I like to think that at this specific moment, in various places in the world, young people are immersed in reading his immortal work."

Hearing that excerpt about the dark forest, TV viewers guess that the mutilated body—they are almost always, and almost always brutally—will be found in an undergrowth. That is often the case. Serial killers lack originality.

And our investigator, the one who leaves no detail unturned, appears. Black turtleneck, jeans, three-day beard, dark hair. Strangely, they resemble one another, the man in the motel and him. Except that the investigator seems younger. But, as we've seen, the age of the former is impossible to determine.

"Well, there you go; they found the little one," the man in the motel—whose name will remain unknown—says. "They took enough time. Finally, they've stopped looking for her. I must tell you I'm happy for the parents. I really was sad for them. I too have a heart. Admit that I hid her well. But I didn't bury her."

Dante Sullivan, nicknamed the jaguar, the name of the character portrayed by Lukas Balta—now studies the scene of the crime, in an undergrowth, in fact, a few hundred metres from a highway in California. A young woman, perhaps twenty-five years old, lies on a carpet of leaves, enucleated, the top of her body bare, breasts severed. Nothing particularly new under the sun. She is not gagged. A few steps away, a pair of glasses with purple frames.

Sullivan and his team search the surroundings for clues, traces of DNA and so on. A cigarette butt is picked up, placed in a plastic bag. Stained blades of grass in other bags. A shoe print is photographed.

The man in the motel knows they won't find anything like that around Fanny. He was very careful. In any case, he never smoked.

Five minutes of advertisements: shampoo, yogurt, Coca-Cola. Always the same. The man in the motel sighs.

A day has passed. Presently, the team of experts is meeting in Sullivan's office. No sexual abuse, announces the medical examiner. The victim died very slowly, after horrendous suffering, bleeding to death. Traces of burns on the entire body, fractured humerus, three broken ribs. And the breasts, the eyes ... Strangled, finally. The profiler gives his opinion. He says that, in his opinion, the perpetrator of the crime had an unhappy childhood. No doubt traumatized by an abusive mother, which explains the removal of the breasts. She refused to breast-feed him or perhaps breastfed him for too long. He couldn't bear her gaze, hence the enucleation. In any case, one thing is certain: the psychopath hates women. He did not gag his victim, because he enjoyed hearing her cries of pain. Luna, the specialist in Internet searches—she does not work on the ground—types this information on the keyboard of her laptop.

The man in the motel shakes his head.

"You lack originality, Dante Sullivan: you're like your characters. According to you, or the people who write your scripts, all psychopaths have had a violent father, a schizophrenic mother or vice-versa. Well, sorry to contradict you, but not me. My childhood was completely normal, ordinary, you could even call it happy. If you can say that children are happy. No one mistreated me, you see: I had a little brother, we had a dog called Kitty — a spaniel with big, sad eyes — a Persian cat, a canary in a cage, three red fish. Dad was an insurance agent; Mom a volunteer at the local library. All on the East Coast. Once at Christmas, we went to Disney World. No, you won't find me by delving into my past. But don't kid yourself, you won't find me."

He drinks a sip of vodka.

Now the team is on the trail of the murderer. He is perhaps in Arizona. Local investigation. A mechanic, a waitress, and a hardware store employee are questioned. A composite drawing is produced. Luna searches in the database for suspects. Various faces, sinister-looking, appear on her screen. The psychologist believes the guilty one suffers from a mental illness: that's where they should investigate. He suggests beginning by looking for patients recently let out or escaped from psychiatric hospitals in the region, then expanding the search, applying it to the entire country — the psychopath has perhaps moved around. Focusing on the fact that they are probably dealing with someone impotent: the victim was not raped.

The man in the motel now looks bored.

"Oh! Mental illness. That's what they still always say when they can't find an explanation. But there's no explanation: stop trying to look for one. The wolf carries the lamb, and then eats him without any other why or wherefore ... You read Dante, jaguar — you were called cougar in the first shows. You're called *couguar* in French and in Spanish you became a *pantera*, when cougar took on a less virile meaning, shall we say. But the French kept *couguar*, and I concur. So you read Dante, but have you read Jean de La Fontaine? *The Wolf and the Lamb*: do you see what I'm talking about? Yes, I speak French. Fortunately, because the little girl's English was rather poor. I also speak Spanish, a bit of Russian: soon I'm going to tackle Mandarin. And I speak Italian, of course. *La Divina Commedia*: I read it in the original. *Lasciate ogne Speranza, voi ch'intrate*. I taught her the sentence at the beginning of the *Inferno*: "Abandon all hope, ye who enter here." She had to declaim it as she entered the cage. Cage! Damn! I've said too much. That won't happen again. But did I say cage or cave? Ha! Your job to find out … In any case, she had a very nice accent.

"So, *The Wolf and the Lamb*. We played that game, Lolita and I. I like calling her Lolita even though her real name was Fanny. The wolf and the lamb—that's how things happen in nature: we can do nothing to change them. The wolf is hungry; the wolf is always hungry. He eats the lamb. That's it, that's all. The strongest one wins. The wolf is not a vegetarian. I made the pleasure last. I am speaking of mine of course, but you'll have understood that.

"And you know what, Dante? You were her idol. We watched a few episodes of your series together, to reward her when she was well-behaved. Because there weren't only punishments: don't think that. I also planned rewards and you were a part of that. Imagine that she wanted to become a profiler, to hunt down pedophiles and serial killers. Or to work in forensics. Can you imagine? For me, that type of role wouldn't work. The bad guys are more fascinating. I wanted, I still want to be Sherlock Holmes' Professor Moriarty. Far more interesting, in my opinion. In any case, I had a good laugh.

"But I'm not a pedophile. Or a serial killer. Not yet. That will come. It's just that Lolita was the first in my collection. For the next victim, inspiration will point her out to me. I have nothing in common with those pathetic characters who always kill the same woman in the same way. I have more imagination. You'll hear tell of me ... Unless Lolita was an isolated experience. A scientific experiment, if you like. I have not yet decided. We will see."

The killer on the program has located his next victim. Same physical type as the first: thin, long brown hair; she too wears glasses. She comes out of a pharmacy, gets in her car, starts the engine. The killer follows her in his car. She parks in a deserted underground parking lot. The music now is more disturbing. When she gets out of the car, he gets out too. He gets in the elevator with her.

Her disappearance is reported to Sullivan's team. The profiler puts forward this hypothesis: the killer's mother was perhaps short-sighted, or an optometrist, ophthalmologist, she sold glasses. They have not found the eyes of the first victim. Perhaps he takes them away, like a trophy.

The man in the motel finishes his glass of vodka and pours himself another.

"Resilience—is that the word I'm looking for? Oh! The resistance of children, especially when they're in good health like Fanny-Lolita, athletic, well-fed, with all the proteins and vitamins specialists recommend. She told me she was a vegetarian. I had her eat pig liver. She refused, at first. She ended up giving in. When you are hungry ... Children are brave, my dear Sullivan. Little by little, she answered my questions. That's how I learned her mother's name, Florence. Which explains my presence here. I'm thinking of the mother. As you see, I can show sensitivity occasionally. Even compassion. I have a heart; I told you so. In the end, the little one resigned herself: she understood that no help would be forthcoming. I did not gag her; I let her shout, but no one could hear. That was the problem. For her, of course, not for me."

Luna has found a plausible suspect. Jake Wallace, forty-one years old, treated for two years in the psychiatric unit of Bellevue Hospital in New York, for psychosis with paranoid delusion. Released last December. Mother an optometrist. In January, he took a bus for Los Angeles; the driver formally identified him. "That's our man," Sullivan said.

"I planned everything, prepared everything with a great deal of care. Of course I didn't know it would be her. But when I saw her, at McDonald's, cheek in her hand, looking so lost in front of her chocolate milkshake ... I recognized her right away. There is no other word. I recognized my nymphet. You know, like when it's love at first sight.

"I could see she had troubles. I approached gently; I certainly didn't want to scare her away. Her main problem was that she had no cell phone to reach her parents. Her mother had bought her one, but her father confiscated for the vacation. Fathers are always stricter. Almost always. I shook my head: of course, fathers are like that. They're gruff, uncouth fellows, not open-minded like mothers. And she'd forgotten the telephone number of the apartment. If she'd had her cell phone, it would have been in the memory. With her accent, her grammar mistakes, I could tell right away that she was a French-speaker. So I spoke to her in her language, a way to instill confidence. I showed her my police badge — yes, I made myself one. It wasn't very difficult; besides, how would she have known it was fake? I told her I knew about her running away, that it was my responsibility to bring her back to the condo. She followed me without question: relieved, I would say. Both naïve and resourceful, resourceful enough to run away, naïve enough to follow a perfect stranger. Did you see how I eluded the surveillance camera? Hat pulled over the eyes, head turned away? I practiced for months. And in all sorts of places: elegant nightclubs, supermarkets, shops, train and bus stations, not to mention banks. Never in the same place. But you already guessed that, right? Besides, I had grey hair. I dyed it black. The next time, I'll be blond or red-haired.

"In the car, she told me she'd forgotten her book by the pool. And what was the nymphet reading? You'll never guess, jaguar or cougar, the nymphet was reading *Lolita*! Isn't that a bit risqué for her age? She replied to me that her mother had agreed; that for her a well-written book can be read at any age.

"She flinched when I left the highway. I told her not to worry, that I knew all the shortcuts. But when she began to really become agitated, I had to stop to give her an injection. Enough to make her sleep until Savannah, where I'd set up my hiding place."

The victim is tied to a tree deep in the woods. The murderer undoes the buttons of her blouse, removes her glasses and takes out a knife.

"Would you like me to tell you everything I subjected her to? I'd rather let you guess. You must have a lot of talent for guessing.

"Some children are never found. Burned, thrown into

rivers or into the sea, a stone around their neck, or else abandoned, like Tom Thumb and his brothers deep in a forest, eaten by wolves. I didn't want that for Lolita-Fanny. I didn't want that for her parents, decent people if I go by what she told me.

"I watch all the movies on the subject, all the TV series. There's no doubt about it, you'll always be my favourite.

"I could have become attached. In a way, she was endearing. Yes, I could have, if I'd wanted to. But I had, as they say, other fish to fry. Or as the French say, *d'autres chats à fouetter*, other cats to whip, which I find more poetic. I say that, but ... why did they whip those poor cats? A mystery. I read that in reality it is not *fouetter*—whipping—but *foutre*—fuck—that we're supposed to understand, and not cats, but pussy. *D'autres chattes à foutre*. Far too vulgar for me. Personally, I really like cats. I spoke to you of our family's Persian cat. Now that I think of it, she was called Lolly, in fact."

The jaguar and his team are on the trail of the murderer. They advance in the undergrowth, silently. A shout of terror sounds in the distance. They advance stealthily. Dante Sullivan draws his revolver.

≈ One hour. The program has just ended. The killer has been arrested, the victim, unbound. *In extremis*, perhaps, as usual, but saved. As the credits roll, we hear the voice of Lukas Balta. *Attend not to the fashion of the torment, Think of what follows.* A clue for the next episode. The man in the motel smiles; that is his favourite quote. He turns off the TV.

"In your series, the guilty are always punished, in *The Divine Comedy* as well. But in life, you know as well as I. So long, jaguar. Until tomorrow."

He stands up, stretches, places the black nylon bag on the floor next to the bed, then turns out the lamp, curls up, fully dressed, one hand beneath the pillow, and falls asleep.

17

The *End of the World*, Night

Reread the life of Byron or Shelley: you will see.

A young poet, for example, who washes dishes and cleans vegetables in the ship's galley.

So long …

STILL ON THE deck, the young poet who washes dishes in the ship's galley writes, seated at a table, a bottle of wine and a glass in front of him.

≈ My dear Tépha,

A strange idea to continue writing to a dead man, you will say. Don't worry: it's my last letter. I promised you one at each change of season. Today is the autumn equinox: here it is.

Let me just tell you about my latest events.

A year ago, or almost, I left Montreal, enthusiastic, agitated. You know it: I already described my trips—France, Andalusia, Corsica, Mallorca. In Seville, I fell madly in love with Manuela. I believed I was; I believed or wanted to believe it was for life. A flamenco dancer: a fantasy. Her black mop of hair, her spirit. I was a happy man—I had the wind in my sails. I learned Spanish.

I forgot Don Juan. That is, I discovered him in Seville. I set out to retrace his steps, or those of Miguel de Mañara, his alter ego, in Calvi. Then, in Mallorca, to retrace other steps; I've forgotten which. As if I'd lost myself on the way. I was filled with a kind of rage; I still am. Still seeking, still restless. Like the Wandering Jew—or Canadian. All the while, in Seville, Manuela was expecting our child.

Provided with a, let us say, generous Canada Council grant, I'd left to write an exemplary work. I was going to reinvent poetry, like Rimbaud before me. But I basically wrote nothing of value: notes scribbled in a journal, nothing eloquent. I'm not proud of myself. My head was elsewhere. Don Juan, his story, took over. After Mañara, I became interested in Byron's *Don Juan*, then in Byron himself. I read his life story, I read his books. I tried to translate him—I sent you a few lines in my second letter, I think. Translation is not an easy art. I became exhausted.

My problem is I compared myself to him. He wrote seventeen cantos of *Don Juan* before he died at thirty-seven—can you imagine, Stéphane?—not to mention *Childe Harold, Sardanapalus, The Corsair*, and others. All that while collecting mistresses, and young lovers perhaps, while committing incest with his sister Augusta —he even had a daughter by her named Medora—while travelling all around the world. It's like, for a musician, comparing yourself to Mozart: you'll never measure up. In the end, jealousy eats away at us. No, we feel, we know we are completely useless.

It was in Venice that he wrote the first four cantos of *Don Juan*. I followed him there. In the port, a white ship was moored, the *End of the World*. I simply had to find a way to come on board. But I hadn't a cent, was flat broke. The Canada Council grant had melted ... like snow in the sunshine: excuse the tired simile. I inquired and yes, incredible luck, they actually needed an assistant cook. Did my predecessor get seasick? In any case, not I. So I've spent the last ten days slicing cucumbers, mincing garlic for tzatziki, helping out with the dishes. My goal was to arrive in Greece and, once there, travel to Missolonghi where Byron died of a fever.

I'll tell you right away: I'm not going to Missolonghi. It is here, in the Aegean Sea that my trip will end. I don't see myself returning to Canada with my blank pages, my notebooks and pockets empty. Nor returning to Seville to assume responsibilities that are beyond me. Nor spending the rest of my life disguised as a kitchen boy slicing cucumbers—Cucurbitaceae are also for the sandwiches that accompany English tea.

If only the *End of the World* could sink like the *Titanic*, which left, as proud as a peacock, Southampton and met its destiny off Terra Nova on the night—I verified—of April 14 to 15, 1912. In third class, there were many who believed they were headed for a better world, a happier life. And the titan sank in the North Atlantic, struck by an iceberg, and all its dreams with it. If only the *End of the World* could go down too. Impassive, the musicians of the orchestra would play their corny tunes, *Broken Wings* and the others—that evening, their performance caused a scandal. People heard yelling, distress calls. Prayers to Yahveh, to Jehovah, Jesus, Allah. A fine spectacular sinking that people still speak of a hundred years later, and, at the bottom of the water, the shipwreck that divers would visit. But an iceberg in the Aegean? I'm dreaming in colour. An iceberg is inconceivable. It would be better to expect a pirate attack. Personally, I have no more time to wait.

Byron was a great swimmer. I, as you know, never learned. No chance that I would come back up to the surface once I have dived.

My daughter was born last month. I will not meet her. I know she is named Lola, that's all. Byron was not a good father to his three daughters. He shut one up in a convent; she died there of typhus at age five. I wouldn't have been a good one either. I'm not made for father-hood, family life, all that. A bad poet, bad lover, bad father. Perhaps I was only a good friend. Was I? Yes and no. A real friend must be sincere; I have not been sincere with you. Your paintings—deep down I called them crap—I never liked them. Too Gauguinesque. You signed them "Tépha;" you believed that's how people would pronounce your name in Polynesia—they did call Gauguin Koké—you dreamed of the Marquesas. You were obsessed by Gauguin the way Byron now obsesses me. Your talent, your genius: I didn't believe in it. Only your Julie believed in it, but love makes people blind, as they say. To support you, the poor thing danced completely nude at the Geisha Bar—or was it Floozie's Bar, I can't remember. I'm being mean now, forgive me. The truth, I'm telling it to you now, I'm telling you straight: you were no better a painter than I am a good poet. We're both losers.

Allow me just one moment of nostalgia, now. You remember the times we got plastered, our crazy nights; you'd often declaim interminable speeches from *Crime and Punishment*. You knew it by heart and I'd recite the *Drunken Boat*, I knew it by heart too; I still do, or almost.

"And from then on I bathed in the Poem of the Sea, infused with stars and lactescent … " Lactescent. How I loved that word, how I envied Rimbaud for daring to write it at age seventeen. Then: "But, in truth, I've wept too much! Dawns are heartbreaking. Every moon is atrocious and every sun bitter. Acrid love has swollen me with intoxicating torpor O let my keel burst! O let me go into the sea!" You cried out *Greetings to you, Arthur Rimbaud!*, and I *Greetings to you, Fyodor Mikhailovich!* And we threw our glasses against the wall. All those bars where the bouncers didn't want to let us in anymore, even when we promised to only drink mineral water. Our behaviour would be exemplary, we'd swear to it. They didn't believe us. How old were we; when was it? Eighteen, twenty years old. Ages ago. I miss the wild times we had. I've become cynical and hard.

The world is too small, Stéphane. The world is too small for me. Or else it is I who am too small for the world.

It's true, the flesh is sad when you've loved books too much. Remember Don Quixote, he also loved them too much; they took him for a madman. The books have all been written, Stéphane; the paintings have all been painted; the music has all been composed. That is our misfortune; that is our tragedy. There's nothing left for us to write, nothing left to paint: we were born too late. I will not go to Abyssinia like Rimbaud, but to the sea, like his boat. I'm almost there. I'll finish this letter and will be there.

I reassure or console myself by telling myself that many artists have died young. Jim Morrison, Kurt Cobain.

Twenty-seven years old, like you, like me. Rimbaud survived, Gauguin too, but in what condition? Weakened, maimed. I won't end up like that.

It wasn't Bryon who drowned himself. It was Shelley. Shelley, you know, the English poet, the husband of Madame Frankenstein. In the Gulf of Spezia, on a stormy day. Always the Mediterranean. Byron was bled to death. That's how they cared for people, in the past. Thought the illness would go away at the same time as the pint or two of blood they siphoned from them. I wonder if the treatment ever healed people, if some survived it. Not Byron. "If thou regret'st thy Youth, *why live*?" he wrote shortly before breathing his last, in Missolonghi.

I regret mine.

He had no more desire to live. Neither do I.

Oh, I've written a poem; I'm attaching it to my letter. But no, it's not worth it. Instead, I'll tear it into tiny pieces and throw it in the water. The fish will feast, do you think? It's a poem about the sea. I'm not the first to be inspired by it, you will say.

I'll place my letter, rolled up very tightly, in a bottle, the Château Margaux that I stole from the reserve—I won't tell you the price, well beyond our means. I delight to think of the psychodrama that will explode when they discover the theft. But out of the question to deny myself this pleasure, this last exquisite delight. Besides, in the evening, Byron would drink two bottles of Bordeaux, apparently.

Then I'll go join him somewhere in the beyond. Join you, rather. There must be a place for misfits like us, a kind of oblivion, I don't know. A place Dante neglected to describe in his *Divine Comedy*. A star, a moon in another galaxy. Elsewhere. An end of the world, if that even exists. But it does exist. *The End of the World Is Elsewhere*, that's the title I'm going to give the collection of poems I did not write.

Well, so long, my friend. *Hasta luego.*

François

* * *

The sound of a sudden splash. Hope Mary gives a start. Something—or someone?—has just fallen into the water, she is sure. William? She turns around, scans the deck, then scans the sea. But the sea is black.

The young man who was writing earlier is no longer there.

Acknowledgements

Note: the translations from Rimbaud's *Drunken Boat* in Chapter 17 are by Wallace Fowlie.

About the Author

Born in Montreal, **Hélène Rioux** has published ten novels, notably *L'amour des hommes* and *Traductrice de sentiments* (*Reading Nijinsky*), short story collections, including *L'homme de Hong Kong* and *Pense à mon rendez-vous* (*Date with Destiny*), narratives and poetry. A literary translator, she has translated seventy works from English and Spanish to French as well as books and picture books for children. Shortlisted six times for the Governor General's Literary Award, she received the Prix Québec et le Prix Ringuet of the Académie des lettres du Québec for *Mercredi soir au Bout du monde* (*Wednesday Night at the End of the World*), the Grand Prix littéraire of the Journal de Montréal and the Prix de la Société des Écrivains canadiens for *Chambre avec baignoire* (*Room with Bath*) and the QSPELL Translation Award for *Self* by Yann Martel. Member of the collectif de redaction of the *XYZ* magazine, she also wrote a column on literary translation in the *Lettres québécoises* journal. In addition to being translated into English, her novels have been translated into Spanish and Bulgarian.

About the Translator

Jonathan Kaplansky won a French Voices Award to translate Annie Ernaux's *La Vie extérieure* for the University of Nebraska Press. His recent publications include Jean-Pierre Le Glaunec's *The Cry of Vertières: Liberation, Memory, and the Beginning of Haiti* and Lise Tremblay's *Chemin Saint-Paul*. He has sat on the juries for the English-translation category of the Governor General's Literary Awards and the John Glassco translation prize. He is currently translating the libretto of an opera written by Hélène Dorion and Marie-Claire Blais: *Yourcenar An Island of Passions* (music by Éric Champagne).

MIX
Paper
FSC® C100212

Printed in March 2022
by Gauvin Press,
Gatineau, Québec